11/11
'7.00

The Point
in the
Market

A Mamur Zapt Mystery

Books by Michael Pearce

The Mamur Zapt Series

The Mamur Zapt and the Return of the Carpet
The Night of the Dog
The Donkey-Vous
The Men Behind
The Girl in the Nile
The Spoils of Egypt
The Camel of Destruction
The Snake-Catcher's Daughter
The Mingrelian Conspiracy
The Fig Tree Murder
The Last Cut
Death of an Effendi
A Cold Touch of Ice
The Face in the Cemetery
The Point in the Market
The Mark of the Pasha

Sandor Seymour Mysteries

A Dead Man in Athens
A Dead Man inn Tangier
A Dead Man in Trieste
A Dead Man in Istanbul

Dimitri and the One-Legged Lady

The Point in the Market

A Mamur Zapt Mystery

Michael Pearce

Poisoned Pen Press

Copyright © 2005 by Michael Pearce

First U.S. Trade Paperback Edition 2006

10 9 8 7 6 5 4 3 2

Library of Congress Catalog Card Number: 2004111094

ISBN: 978-1-59058-297-8 Trade Paperback

Poisoned Pen Press
6962 E. First Ave., Ste. 103
Scottsdale, AZ 85251
www.poisonedpenpress.com
info@poisonedpenpress.com

Printed in the United States of America

Chapter One

'Effendi, Effendi, there is excitement!' panted the small boy. 'Over there in the Camel Market!'

The small boys had already done pretty well out of Owen that morning. They had found a body tucked beneath the carpeting of a fiki's booth and had pointed it out to him with relish. He had told them to find a policeman, at which they had been a little surprised, for they had been under the impression that he *was* a policeman. However, they had readily proceeded to the obvious explanation that the Mamur Zapt was too grand a chap to be bothered with ordinary bodies and had run off to find one of the constables patrolling the Market.

Then they had found a dead baby lying among the fodder for the camels and had tried that out on him but with a similar lack of success.

And now there was this 'excitement,' whatever it was. There did indeed seem to be something going on over on the other side of the Market and he went across.

There was a ring of men, growing larger with every minute, and in the middle of the ring was a donkey and two men. One of the men was a Levantine, dressed in a dark suit and wearing a tarboosh, the little, pot-like red hat which was the Egyptian badge of office; the other an ordinary fellah in the usual blue gown. They seemed to be arguing.

noyed, because if this was all it was then one
nstables ought to have been able to sort it out,
hree of them in the crowd, just standing by
But then he saw that there were some soldiers
' part of the crowd but formed in a separate
wondered what the hell was going on.

'But I didn't bring him in to sell him!' cried the villager, almost
weeping. 'I was going to take him to the barber, that's all!'

'That's right,' said the donkey-barber, standing in the front
row of the crowd and recognisable by the clippers in his hand
and the pile of clippings at his feet. 'He'd just got to me.'

'He's here, isn't he?' said the Levantine. 'And we need him.'

'But I need him too!' cried the villager. 'Brothers,' he appealed
to the crowd, 'I need a donkey to work my land!'

'You don't need a donkey,' said one of the constables helpfully. 'You need a buffalo.'

'Yes, but I haven't *got* a buffalo. I can't afford one. So I use
a donkey.'

'Sell the donkey and buy a buffalo,' said the Levantine, taking
out a bundle of notes and waving them in front of the villager's
nose. 'With this!'

The villager's eyes followed the notes hypnotically.

'How much is that?' he whispered.

'Fifty piastres. Fifty whole piastres! Buy a buffalo!'

The villager recoiled.

'It wouldn't buy a buffalo!'

'It wouldn't buy a donkey, either,' said one of the villagers
behind him. 'Don't have anything to do with it, Ibrahim.'

'I won't!'

'I don't have to buy,' said the Levantine, nettled. 'I can just
take.'

'I'd like to see you!'

'Just try it!' said one of the villagers.

The constables shifted uneasily. The soldiers, who were
Egyptians, ostentatiously fingered their rifles.

There were some Australian soldiers among the crowd, disembarked and here in the Market sightseeing.

'Hey!' said one of them. 'You can't do that! Take the man's donkey. Just like that!'

'I have powers to commandeer,' said the Levantine smoothly. 'We need both. Camels for the Camel Corps, donkeys for the Transport Corps. We pay compensation. It's a fair price."

The Australians looked at each other.

'If it's for the Army…'

'And a fair price….'

'It's not a fair price!' cried the villager. 'He was paying seventy five in the village!'

'And that's not a fair price, either,' said one of the villagers. 'A hundred would be about right.'

The Levantine shrugged.

'Seventy five is all I am empowered to offer,' he said, 'and that only for a really good animal. It's a fair price and the one I agreed with your omda,' he said to the villager.

'Seventy five plus the bribe you paid to the omda,' said one of the villagers bitterly.

The Levantine appeared not to hear him.

'All right,' he said to the obstinate donkey-owner. 'I'll make that fifty into seventy five. That's fair, isn't it?' he appealed to the crowd.

'No,' said the donkey-owner, 'I want to keep my donkey.'

'That,' warned the Levantine, 'or nothing.'

'I need my donkey.'

'Nothing, then.'

The Levantine made a sign with his hand and the Egyptian soldiers moved forward.

The crowd behind the villager surged. Some of the men were holding sticks, others, stones.

'Hey—' began one of the Australians.

The soldiers stopped. Villagers were one thing, Australians another.

Owen pushed his way through the crowd.

, 'that will do!'

 twitched to attention and stepped forward.

 ower to requisition animals on a private basis,'

Levantine. 'It must be done through the vil-

 Levantine.

'Take your donkey and go,' Owen said to the villager. 'Quickly!'

The man needed no urging. He seized the donkey, perched himself feet up on its back, and headed off.

The Levantine shrugged and turned away. Owen could see now that he had assembled quite a substantial herd over beyond the makeshift tents.

The Camel Market itself was almost empty, denuded of virtually all its stock. Only a couple of sucking mothers were left with their infants. One of them was no more than a day old, still a fluffy little white ball. Owen couldn't see how something so endearing could grow up into the ugly, morose, bloody-minded beast that it did. But, of course, he reflected, some might say that was true of human beings too.

The crowd was dispersing now, going back to the rows of figures squatting on the bare earth behind their heaps of corn, cucumbers, or onions, or crouched beneath ragged pieces of cloth stretched between sticks, selling kohl bottles, lurid cottons, copper pots, or the celluloid beads, scarlet to suggest the coral of Bedawin jewellery, favoured of the herdsmen.

Owen felt a touch on his arm. It was one of the Australians.

'We're looking for the Wagh el Birket,' he said.

I'll bet, thought Owen. The Wagh was one of the most notorious districts of Cairo.

'You're quite a bit out of your way,' he said. 'If I were you, I'd take an arabeah. Over there!'

There was a row of them, little, open-fronted, single-horse drawn carriages, the taxi of Cairo, fly-blown, worn, and smelling strongly of horse urine. The six Australians somehow succeeded in piling into two of them.

'Ten piastres,' Owen called after them. 'Don't pay more!'

They would. The Australians had only started arriving in Egypt a month ago but they were already wildly popular because of their open-handedness. Not just, to be fair, their open-handedness. There was a general openness about them. They talked in natural, easy terms to the Egyptians, without any of the stiffness or distancing of the British. They were a breath of fresh air, Owen reflected.

He looked around him. The Market was quiet now. He walked across it for one last time and then headed for his office, leaving behind him the Levantine with his herds, the figures crouched behind their piles of vegetables or huddled beneath their makeshift tents, the small boys playing now in the empty spaces of the Camel Market, throwing camel pellets at each other, the baby in the berseem, and the body beneath the carpeting of the fiki's booth.

∽

The war was in its sixth month now and the slouch hats of the Australians were not the only thing that was different on the streets of Cairo. Prices had risen sharply, especially the prices of basic things, like paraffin, which was widely used in the poorer quarters for cooking. Ordinary people were complaining bitterly; and yet Cairo seemed well to do as never before. The shops in the Ismailiya, the fashionable European quarter, were doing a roaring trade. The great hotels were full. Normally—that is, as Owen was learning to say, before the war—at this time of year, when the Cairo Season had just about ended, they would be half empty.

But although they were full, he reflected as he sat in the Long Bar at Shepheard's that evening with Curtis, they were full with a different sort of people. Instead of the bright young things in bright new dresses, fresh out from England, and their circles of swains, drawn chiefly from the officers messes of the various British garrisons, tailored a little too perfectly to be ordinary human beings, the place was full of businessmen. It was hard to find an unoccupied corner. Which was why he had got landed with Curtis.

He had discovered a sofa and arm-chair behind some potted palms and had settled down to wait for Zeinab. Zeinab was, as usual, late, and when Curtis had appeared through the palms and asked anxiously if he might…? Owen had had no alternative but to agree with grace. Curtis, pink-faced and pink-ginned, had slid into the chair opposite and then, unfortunately, proceeded to engage him in conversation.

This was, perhaps, fair enough, except that Curtis had insisted on talking about work, first his own—he had come out from England, he told Owen, to help manage Supplies (whatever they might be)—and then, at too great length, about Owen's, about which he knew very little but had melodramatic notions.

'I suppose you're here on duty?' he said.

'Well, um—'

'Got to keep an eye of them. They're everywhere.'

'Ye-es?'

'Spies.' He looked around meaningfully.

Owen's heart sank. That was another of the changes that had overtaken the city. Whereas before the war people had talked about sex and sport, now they talked about spies.

He looked across the vestibule at the dark-suited business-men.

'I don't know,' he said. 'I think they're mostly just people on the make.'

'Don't I know it!' said Curtis. 'Remember, I have to deal with them!' He leaned forward towards Owen and dropped his voice:

'But is that true of all of them? That Greek, for instance—he looks a shady customer.'

'They're all shady,' said Owen.

'Don't I know it! You can't do a thing here without a bit of—' He nodded his head significantly and rubbed the tip of his finger against his thumb. 'Even the Government offices!'

Owen felt moved to defend the offices.

'You're got to see it as they do,' he said. 'It's not so much a bribe as a present. It changes the nature of the relationship. Moves it from being purely commercial to something more friendly. Less cold, less hard, more personal. They find us very abstract and distant.'

He suddenly thought of the Levantine and the villager's donkey. That hadn't been very abstract or friendly.

Curtis was nodding his head.

'I know,' he said, touching finger to thumb once more. 'It smoothes the way.'

Owen sighed inwardly.

'But it's not that so much,' said Curtis, looking round again. 'It's the talk! No one here's got any idea of keeping his mouth shut about things. You don't need to bribe them—they'll spill it out anyway! Cairo leaks like a sieve.'

That was certainly true. It always had been. If you wanted to find out what the Cabinet had discussed that morning, or what the Consul-General had said to the Khedive—sorry, High Commissioner to Sultan—that had changed, too, or, indeed, what you had said to your wife in private last night, then the place to go was the Bazaar area.

'Take that man, for instance,' said Curtis, looking at Abdul, the bartender. 'I'll bet he could tell you a thing or two.'

Owen hoped he could. That was what he paid him for. Although, of course, others might be paying him as well.

'And what he can hear, others can,' said Curtis. 'I'll bet there's more than a few of them in here. I must say, I don't envy you your job. They're everywhere!'

Owen glanced at his watch. Where the hell was Zeinab?

'The trouble is,' confided Curtis, 'that there are so many foreigners here. It's not like at home. You can't trust people.' He looked balefully at the inoffensive Greek, who seemed deep in a conversation about cotton futures. 'Even the Egyptians. *Especially* the Egyptians. They're all pro-Turk. And what's bad is that so many of them are in influential places.'

Zeinab at last appeared, tall, slender, and veiled, as was usual with Egyptian women.

'My wife,' said Owen.

❦

They were going on to a reception at the British Agency given to mark the arrival of the new High Commissioner, and Owen was feeling nervous. It would be the first public engagement he had taken Zeinab to since she had become his wife, and he wasn't sure how that, or Zeinab, would be received. There was a social divide in Egypt between the British and the Egyptians. Members of the British Administration didn't marry Egyptians. Except that Owen had.

They were ushered up the steps by Cavasses dressed in splendid scarlet and gold and then into the ballroom. The new Commissioner, MacMahon, was standing just inside the door to receive them.

The Senior Cavass announced the guests as they appeared.

'The Mamur Zapt and—' he hesitated: this was a new one—'Mrs Mamur Zapt,' he recovered confidently.

The Oriental Secretary was standing by MacMahon's side, muttering explanations.

'Captain Owen. Head of the Sultan's Secret Police. And Mrs Owen. Mrs Owen is the daughter of Nuri Pasha, a former Minister of Justice and a very old friend of ours.'

MacMahon bent forward and greeted Zeinab warmly. They moved on.

Owen knew exactly what Paul Trevelyan had done, and was grateful. By establishing the terms on which the High Commissioner had received Zeinab, he had made it difficult for other people to do otherwise.

He helped Zeinab to a glass from the tray proffered by a red-fezzed, red-sashed suffragi, took one for himself, and then looked around. Over by the French windows a very tall man with a booming Scottish voice was talking to an elderly Egyptian woman. There weren't many Egyptian women at the reception but Labiba Latifa was exceptional in more ways than one. She was the widow of a former Dean of the Medical School and well known in Cairo society for her charitable work, especially in the field of public health. The man was Cairns-Grant, the senior pathologist at the Hospital and himself internationally known. Owen took Zeinab across to them.

'Zeinab!' said Latifa, taking her hands in her own, 'I was so delighted when I heard!'

'So ye've married?' said Cairns-Grant. 'Well, it's a good thing for both of you. You'll live longer, did ye know that?'

This was the easy bit. The medical community stood to some extent on its own, outside the normal British community, and relations with Egyptians were not subject to the same constraints.

While they were talking, he considered his next step.

Cunningham, the Financial Adviser, had come in with his wife just before Owen and was standing apart from the others. Cunningham was the senior British official after the High Commissioner. In a society as hierarchical as the British expatriate community, this mattered. It meant that, in the absence of MacMahon's wife, his wife set the tone for the British society.

He took Zeinab across and introduced her.

He saw Mrs Cunningham studying her. The women, he thought, would be harder than the men. He could see she couldn't quite make Zeinab out. The veil concealed her features. She wasn't the only woman in the room wearing a veil with European dress—there were a number of Diplomatic wives—and she spoke perfect French and English.

'I'm Margaret,' Mrs Cunningham said suddenly.

'Zeinab.'

They went on talking for several minutes but he couldn't quite tell: had she cooled?

He felt a sudden surge of resentment. Who or what was Mrs Cunningham? It wasn't even as if Cunningham was superior to him. Owen was the Head of the Sultan's Secret Police, not of the High Commissioner's.

Unless that was another thing that had changed when England had unilaterally declared a Protectorate.

Some other people joined them and then after a while the Cunninghams moved out into the garden.

The line had stopped coming in now. MacMahon had moved away from the door and was talking to Prince Faruq, one of the Sultan's brothers. The Sultan himself, of course, wasn't there. Faruq was representing him. Owen didn't know Faruq. He had been out of the country for a while.

Paul Trevelyan materialised beside them.

'Hello, Zeinab! Lovely to see you. Can I borrow you for a moment! There's someone I'd like you to meet.'

He took her over to MacMahon and Faruq.

Again Owen felt grateful. There was no hesitation about Paul. Once he'd made up his mind to go down a certain route, there was no turning back. Zeinab was his friend and the wife of his friend and he would see she was bound in, no matter the Mrs Cunninghams.

MacMahon moved away, leaving Faruq and Zeinab. They were deep in conversation. Owen wondered if they had known each other in the past. It was unlikely, since when Faruq had last been in the country, Zeinab would probably have been still in harem. But not impossible. Her father had once moved in such circles.

Faruq moved closer to Zeinab. It was the Arab way, Arabs could hardly talk unless they were touching each other. All the same, Owen felt a flicker of uneasiness. Faruq had a reputation as a womaniser.

Zeinab edged away. Owen began to drift across the room towards them.

He was forestalled by Paul, who in a minute had somehow bestowed Faruq on the Cunninghams—that would be a treat for him!—and got Zeinab talking to the director of the National Opera House. Zeinab was fond of opera and knew Lamoretti. They were soon talking happily.

Again, Owen felt grateful; but he also felt that uneasiness again. What was Paul up to? Why had he introduced Zeinab to Faruq in the first place? Was he, perhaps, trying to bind him in, too?

When, soon after the start of the war, the British had deposed the Khedive because of his pro-Turk sympathies and declared a protectorate over Egypt, they had installed in his place a man from a different branch of the ruling family, Hussein, in whom they felt more confidence. But with the man had come the family, about whose members much less was known. Perhaps all that Paul was trying to do was make sure of them, and using Zeinab for that purpose. If that was all it was, Owen didn't mind. Up to a point.

She seemed to be getting on all right now, the centre of an admiring group from the French Consulate. To the French, he thought cynically, the fact that she was a pretty woman mattered much more than her nationality. How did the British get to be so wrong?

He went out on to the balcony. Through the bougainvillaea, bright with red and pink, he could see the Nile sparkling in the sun. Feluccas were tacking to and fro and a little group had gathered at the end of the garden to watch them.

Someone raised a hand. It was Lawrence, a little, fair-haired man, who before the war had been an archaeologist and now was something in Intelligence. He was talking to the new Sirdar. Maxwell, new, that was, in terms of occupancy of the post of Commander in Chief, but not, God be praised, in terms of Egypt.

'Owen's the chap you want to talk to, if that's what you're worried about,' he said to Maxwell, and then moved off.

'What are you worried about, Conky?' asked Owen.

'Drink,' said Maxwell. 'The bloody Australians. They drink like fishes. At any one time half the army's unconscious and the other half's incapacitated with a hangover. What if the Turks come over the Canal? I'll be on my bloody own!'

'I don't think I'd worry too much,' said an Australian officer standing nearby. 'Australians have a great capacity for fighting. Drunk or sober. Drunk, perhaps, especially.'

'I'd just like to be sure they could stand up if need be. Can't you do something about it?' he said to Owen. 'Shut down the liquor houses or something?'

'I'm afraid not,' said Owen, 'they're all owned by foreigners.'

And under the peculiarities of the Egyptian legal system, foreigners were virtually safe from prosecution. They could unduly insist on being tried by their own Consular courts and in a place as far away from Egypt as possible. The police could not even enter their premises without the permission of their consuls, much less close them down.

'That right?' said the Australian officer.

'Gambling dens, too,' said Owen.

'Jesus, they've certainly got it worked out here!'

'The trouble is, it affects the condition of the men,' said a British Officer primly.

'It's not so much that,' said another officer. 'It's the security aspect.'

'Oh, God,' said Owen. 'Not spies again!'

'You may laugh, Owen, but it's a serious matter. Other ranks go to these places—'

'Officers don't go there too?' asked the Australian innocently.

Owen found himself warming to him.

'I think you need to be aware, Connolly,' said the British Officer, jaw set, 'that Cairo leaks like a sieve. Let slip something, and the next moment it's all round the place. You can't depend on people's loyalty, you see. They're all foreigners—'

'They are?'

'Cairo's got more foreigners than any other city in the world. One eighth of the population is foreign-born. Did you know that, sir?' he said, turning to Maxwell. 'I came across the fact yesterday. One eighth! It gives you some idea,' he said, addressing Connolly again, 'of our difficulties.'

'Well, I don't know—'

'All sorts. Greeks. Italians. Serbians. Montenegrins. Syrians. Armenians. Moroccans. Tunisians. Maltese—'

'British?' suggested the Australian.

'They're not the ones I'm worried about,' said Maxwell. 'They've been here a long time and whatever allegiances they have, they're not usually to the other side. No, what worries me is the Turkish element. You see,' he said to Connolly, 'before we took over, Egypt was part of the Ottoman Empire. Been so for centuries. The Khedives were Turks. So were the Pashas. The whole Egyptian ruling class is still largely Turkish. The officers in the Army are Turkish. The police inspectors are Turkish. So are the mudirs, the local governors. Broadly, anyone who tells someone else what to do, is Turkish. Except when he's British, of course.'

'Turks everywhere,' said the British officer.

'And which way they'll jump when the Turks cross the Canal—'

'We're in enemy territory,' said the British officer. 'Virtually.'

'Just a minute,' said the Australian. 'Let's get this straight. You've got all these foreigners in Egypt, Armenians, Montenegrins and so on. You've got the ruling classes, who are Turkish. You've got the British here in droves, running the place. Now where the hell in all this are the Egyptians?'

⁊⊙⊙⊙

Owen went up the front steps of the Bab el Khalk, the police headquarters, and in at the main door. He passed the orderly office, with all its bearers, exchanging salaams with the man on duty, and then climbed up the steps to the top corridor, which was where he had his office. As he walked along the corridor, he passed the offices of Garvin, the Commandant of the Cairo Police, due for retirement but asked to stay on, and McPhee, the eccentric Deputy Commandant. In the past these posts had both been held by Turks; but these days it was the British who told the Turks who told the...

At the end of the corridor, round a corner and slightly separate from the main building, was the office of the Special Secret Clerk, Nikos. Nikos was a Copt. The Copts had been in Egypt since the time of the Pharaohs and looked on the Arabs as foreigners too. And for about the whole of that time they had been embedded in the bureaucracy. They were masters of the arts of managing administrative information, and Owen sometimes surmised that, behind it all, they were the real rulers of Egypt.

Owen nodded 'good morning' to Nikos and went on through to his own office. As he passed Nikos, the Copt looked up.

'Sabri is dead,' he said.

Owen stopped.

'Sabri?'

The name was familiar.

'One of our men,' said Nikos. 'He was out at Farafreh.'

'What was he doing there?'

'Getting camels.'

Owen came back into the room.

'Did he get them?'

'Oh, yes.'

'Where did he die?'

'Here.'

'What did he die of?'

'He was stabbed.'

'A quarrel?'

'I don't know yet. The Parquet are looking into it.'

'Well, well.' It was not unusual for his agents to die. Nor even unusual for them to be stabbed in quarrels, particularly if they were Bedawin or rode with the Bedawin. All the same...

'We need to look into this,' he said.

'It happened at the Camel Market,' said Nikos. 'Yesterday.'

'Yesterday? At the Camel Market? I was there.'

He suddenly remembered.

'Was the body found in a fiki's booth?'

'That's right,' said Nikos, surprised.

Owen thought.

'Are we looking after the family?' he said.

'I'll see to them.'

Agents were not exactly Government employees so their widows were not entitled to a pension. Nevertheless, Owen liked to do something for the family if he could, especially if they had been killed on Government business. But was that the case this time?

'We need to look into this,' he said.

Chapter Two

'Leaks like a sieve,' said the Army representative, looking at Owen accusingly.

Overhead, the huge fan whirled silently, stirring the papers on the table. The French windows leading into the Residency garden were open, as was the door into the corridor, to secure a through draught. There had been some argument about that. 'I thought these meetings were supposed to be secret?' the Army man had said. 'Which would you prefer?' Paul Trevelyan had said wearily. 'Secrecy, or not to die of heat?' The meeting had elected for survival.

'That's hardly Owen's fault,' said Cavendish. Cavendish was chairing.

'Well, I know,' said the Army, 'but isn't he supposed to be doing something about it?'

'There's nothing you can do about it,' said Beevor. 'Given the nature of the country.'

Beevor was rather older than the rest of them. He was another ex-archaeologist and before the War he had travelled extensively in the Near East.

'Yes, but at the moment it's impossible to do anything without the enemy knowing. We had a convoy going out to Kantara yesterday and some of the trucks lost their way. They stopped to ask where they were. "You want Kantara," said some ragged urchin playing in the gutter. "First left!"'

'Egypt is a very open country,' said Owen. 'You can't hope to keep things secret.'

'Yes, but, Christ,' said the Army representative, 'that means that Johnny Turk will know exactly where we're concentrating our troops!'

'If it's any consolation,' said Lawrence, who was also a member of the Committee, 'we know exactly where he's concentrating his troops, too.'

It was all right, but he was a bit too fond, thought Owen, of reminding other people of how good he was.

'Maybe,' said the Army man sharply, 'but—'

That's what always happened. The little, fair-haired man always rubbed people up the wrong way.

'We can all see the problem,' said Cavendish swiftly, smoothing it over. 'But that's the nature of war out here, I'm afraid.'

'Anyway,' said Owen, 'they're just as likely to be getting false information as they are true information.'

Paul laughed; then began to tap his pencil thoughtfully. Around his hand, as it rested on the blotter, a large damp smudge began to spread out from his sweat.

'Couldn't we build on that?' he said.

Cavendish looked at him quickly.

'What do you mean?' he said.

'Issue more false information?' said the Army representative bitterly. 'We've got enough of that as it is!'

'We can't hope to conceal things completely,' said Paul. 'I agree with you, the place leaks like a sieve. But maybe we can deceive the Turks about our intentions.'

'Some form of decoy?'

'Roughly, yes. Establish a false base. Or maybe more than one. At any rate it would plant a seed of doubt in their minds.'

There were nods all round the table and it was agreed that the Army would create dummy bases on the Egyptian side of the Canal.

'But that won't be enough,' said Cavendish. 'It needs to be backed up by other things. Roads, depots. False movements, fake paper-work. Misinformation.' He looked at Owen. 'Deliberate leaks?'

'Owen ought to be good at that,' said Lawrence. 'He seems to have such difficulty in stopping them.'

The meeting of the Committee, which was the country's senior intelligence-gathering body, had taken place at the British Residency. Not at the Abdin Palace, where the Sultan had his office and where his Prime Minister held Cabinet meetings. Nor at any of the large Ministerial buildings which Owen could see from the garden as he came out. Which said something, he reflected, about the location of power in Egypt.

In a way there was nothing new about that. For thirty years a British Adviser had stood at the elbow of every Minister, just as the Consul-General himself had stood beside the Prime Minister shaping everything he did. But although that had been the reality, the British had been careful to preserve the forms: they were, they maintained, in Egypt as advisers only, assisting an independent, fully sovereign Government.

And it hadn't been completely a pretence, thought Owen. There had always been an obligation to work through the formal system. It was the Minister who signed things and not the Adviser. And in that obligation had lain a kind of recognition. He himself, for instance, had always seen himself as working for the Khedive, as the ruler had then been called, and only incidentally for the British; resolving any discrepancies between the two by telling himself that he worked for Egypt.

The declaration of a British Protectorate over Egypt, and the brutal replacement of the ruler by one more sympathetic to British interest, had changed all that. What had been veiled was now unveiled; and it forced not only British officials like Owen to confront uncomfortable truths, but also, and much more importantly, the Egyptians.

As Owen was crossing the street, he heard the violent clanging of a bell and one of the new fire engines dashed out from the

main fire brigade station just off the Ataba-el-Khadra. 'Dash' is
perhaps putting it a little strongly since the engine was drawn
by four cart-horses specially imported from England for the
purpose. The cart-horses, much larger than the usual Egyptian
horse, were new in Cairo and people, including Owen, drew
aside to look. The horses pounded off in the general direction
of Ezbekiya Square.

Owen continued on his way back to the Bab-el-Khalk. He
had just reached the junction with el Torba when he saw an
Englishman coming towards him on a little white donkey. It
was McPhee, the Deputy Commandant of Police. He seemed
in a hurry.

'Fire,' he called to Owen as he went past.

'Want any help?' McPhee wouldn't ordinarily be going to
a fire.

'Possibly,' he called back over his shoulder. 'Wagh el Birket.
Soldiers.'

Owen hurried after him. Behind him he heard another bell
and a moment later another fire engine passed him.

Soon he could see the smoke ahead of him. It billowed up
in a large dark cloud above the houses.

Already the streets were full of people running in that direction. Blocking up the streets, of course, so that nothing could
get through. It was a good job the fire engines had had a start
on them.

Now he could smell the fire and occasionally, in the dark
heavy cloud of smoke, he could see sparks. When he rounded
a corner he could see flames.

It wasn't actually in the Wagh el Birket itself but in one of the
little streets off it. That would make it harder for the firemen.
Still, there would be water nearby in the Ezbekiya Gardens.

He came to a stop. The street ahead was totally blocked with
people. That was the way of things in Cairo. Anything like this
was treated as a public spectacle. Still, they wouldn't just be
watching, there'd be plenty of people there to help.

If they didn't get in the way. That was another thing. People would be milling about all over the place, eager to help, no doubt, but making things difficult for the firemen. Crowd control became important on occasions like this. McPhee would be doing his best but it would be better if he had a few people helping him.

He tried to force a way through the dense press of people but it was solid. He scanned the street in front. He was taller than most of the people in the crowd and could see over their heads. A little way up, on the left, there was what seemed to be a small passage going off at right angles. He pressed himself against the wall and began to work his way along. It took frustratingly long but at last he managed it and dived into the passage. There were people in that, too, but not so many and he was able to push through them.

It was dark in the passage but ahead he could see a glow and when he came to it, he found an even smaller passage, hardly a passage, more a ditch, going off to his right. It was filled with a strange, flickering red light and at the end he could see flames.

He could feel the heat even before he got there. It almost seemed to singe his hair. The end of the passageway was blocked, too, by people but beyond them he could see the house.

The whole front of it was blackened and the wooden, box-like meshrebiya windows had burned away and dropped out, leaving gaping holes. Inside he could see tongues of flame. There was a sudden roar and they leaped up.

The front of the house seemed to tremble and the people in the street cried out. The street was packed solid.

'For Christ's sake!' shouted Owen. 'Get away!'

He shouted again in Arabic. No one heard him. The roar of the fire was too loud.

He tried to force his way through the people standing at the end of the passage but couldn't.

'Make way! Make way!' he shouted, but no one moved or, perhaps could move.

He shouted again, impatiently.

And then an arm reached out of the darkness and grabbed him.

'Effendi! This way!'

'Selim—'

It was one of the constables from the Bab-el-Khalk. There was a door there and he was pulling Owen through.

'Follow me, Effendi!'

He ran up some stairs. The doors off it were open and the rooms were lit with the same lurid red light that he had noticed earlier. There were people in them clustered up against the windows.

Selim went on past them and they came out on to the roof into the usual roof-top garden with its flowers and its jasmine and its runner beans. There were people here, too, standing looking at the house opposite.

Down in the street he could see McPhee. He had some constables with him and they were trying to push the crowd back away from the house and out of the street altogether. But, of course, it was difficult, with the people packed in so tightly behind them.

The flames flickered again and the whole house seemed to be quivering. He could see now that there were jets of water playing on the flames and, following them down, he could see the firemen, in their helmets looking oddly English.

'Can I get down to them?' he asked Selim.

Selim look doubtful.

'The floor above—'

'That'll do.'

It was the harem room. There was a flutter as he went in.

He heard Selim mutter: 'This is the life!'

The women were standing in the huge box window looking out through the lattice work. The wood was hot to the touch. He found a place where he could put his head through, and leaned out.

'McPhee!' he shouted. 'The horses! Use the horses!'

McPhee didn't hear him at first, then didn't understand. But then he nodded and ran to the fire engines. He had difficulty in making clear what he wanted but then one of the men, a driver, probably, unfastened the horses and began to lead them towards the crowd. The constables fell in alongside them.

The crowd fell back, but only by a yard. The constables began to press in on them again. The driver was having difficulty keeping the horses' heads to the crowd. The people wanted to withdraw but couldn't.

The fire roared again and this time some pieces fell off from one of the upper storeys. One of the firemen stopped and gazed at them, fascinated. The pieces fell into the crowd and someone cried out.

The crowd surged but then swayed back to where it had been. People began to scream.

Then, above the uproar, he heard someone shouting commands. It was a man he had not noticed before, standing beside the firemen, dressed like them in fireman's uniform but with a fezz on his head instead of a helmet. One of the jets came off the building and began to play on the people at the end of the street.

They began to retreat. The jet followed them. Foot by foot they were forced back. The people already in front of the house began to move into the space vacated. They in turn were subjected to the jet and, gradually, little by little, the street in front of the burning building was cleared.

❦

Eventually, the fire was brought under control. The hose pipes were turned off and the fire engines used temporarily to block off the ends of the street. The constables with their truncheons dealt with anyone who tried to squeeze past.

McPhee was checking for possible casualties. A number of people had been in the house but they seemed to have got out before the fire took hold. They were sitting in a little subdued group on the ground beneath the overhanging windows of the house opposite. People were bringing them water.

Among them were three Australian soldiers.

'I don't know, mate,' one of them was saying to McPhee. He shook his head bewilderedly. 'I don't know.'

The firemen had taken off their helmets and were sitting exhausted on the ground. Owen went up to the man who had given the orders to clear the street.

'That was well done,' he said.

The man inclined his head in acknowledgement.

'Some things are in the training manual,' he said with a grin. 'Some things are not.'

He was a short, wiry man in late middle age. His hair was grey.

'And some men know what to do when the manual falls silent,' said Owen, 'and others don't.'

The fireman shrugged, pleased.

'It flared up,' he said. 'We were nearly too late.'

'Even with the new horses?'

'They did well. But we will do even better when the new motor-powered engine gets brought in.'

'Motor power?' said Owen, impressed.

'Only one. At the moment. But, still, it will make a difference.'

'There will still be the people.'

'Ah, yes,' said the fireman. 'But this is Cairo!'

He glanced behind him at the fire-blackened building. Wisps of smoke were still curling out from it and a smell of scorching was strong in the air.

'Do you know what made it flare up?' he said. 'It was the spirit. This was a liquor house.'

He shook his head.

'If people only led the lives that God commands,' he said, 'perhaps my men and I would not be necessary.'

He looked at the ruin again.

'It is hard,' he said, 'not to see it as a punishment.'

࿐

Owen chose the same spot again, behind the palm plants.

It was a mistake.

Curtis appeared again and hovered.

'Do you mind? Everywhere else seems to have been taken.'

'Please.' Owen gestured towards the sofa.

Curtis still hesitated.

'Not waiting for your...wife?'

'No, I'm not waiting for my wife,' said Owen, without the pause.

Curtis allowed himself to settle down onto the sofa.

'Work, I expect,' he said.

Owen didn't answer directly.

'And you,' he said.

'Oh, work. In a way.'

He looked round at the businessmen packing the huge foyer, their drinks on the low tables behind them, their heads bent confidentially forwards, talking earnestly in small groups.

'I'm hoping to meet a certain supplier.' He turned back to Owen. 'He doesn't seem to be here yet.'

'What particular line?'

'Building materials. They're establishing some new bases on the Canal.' He gave Owen a quick look. 'Perhaps I shouldn't say that,' he said. 'Not in a place like this. It's still fairly secret.'

'Just came out?'

'That's right. In fact, it's not really out yet. But in Purchasing you tend to get wind of such things early. Especially when it's something this size.'

'Big, is it?'

'Oh, yes. Well, it has to be, doesn't it? With the Turks just the other side of the Canal.'

'It's a long stretch to defend.'

'That's why it has to be several bases. The trouble with that is that it means there has to be a big build-up in purchasing too and the sort of things soon gets noticed. Especially by these chaps here.' He nodded significantly in the direction of the businessmen. 'I try to keep my end quiet but—' he lowered his voice—'not everyone does the same.'

'Place leaks like a sieve.'

'It does. And the problem is, you see,'—he bent forward until his head was almost touching Owen's—'these chaps are all foreigners. We're increasingly having to buy from abroad. They come here and do some business with us and then they go home again!'

'Taking information?'

'That's right! They keep their ears open while they're here and then they go home and, well—' he touched finger against thumb—'it means money. If it's sold in the right place.' He nodded significantly.

'And that's even without the spies?'

'Oh, they're all spies. One way or another.'

He looked balefully at the next table. The unfortunate Greek who had attracted his hostility before was sitting there again. The Greek felt the weight of Curtis' gaze and looked up, then looked away again.

'If they're not already in the enemy's pay, they know how to make money out of it.'

'I daresay you're right.'

The Greek got up from the table and began to go round the groups shaking hands.

Owen looked at his watch.

'If you'll excuse me—'

'Of course, of course!'

Owen stood up.

'You're absolutely right,' he said. 'The place leaks like a sieve. Glad you're taking precautions.'

⟡

The Greek came down the hotel steps, waved away the donkey-boys and the flower-sellers, glanced momentarily at the pornographic pictures pinned to the terrace railings, and then set off down one of the side streets. After a moment Owen followed him.

At this time of day, in the heat, there were few people about, although the tall buildings almost touching overhead made the street a dark corridor of coolness; so dark, in fact, that for a second Owen lost sight of the Greek in the shadows. Then he saw him again, poised at the entrance to an underground Arab coffee house. The Greek disappeared inside.

Owen went down the steps. There was the usual large room with a stone bench running round the wall and low stone tables. In one corner some men were smoking bubble pipes. There was a pleasing gurgle from the water bowls at their feet. The smell of tobacco mingled with the smell of charcoal and with the heavy aroma of coffee and the sweet, sickly smell of hashish.

The Greek was nowhere to be seen, but then Owen made out that there was an inner, lower room which had escaped him in the darkness. The Greek was sitting alone at a table taking off his tie.

Owen sat down opposite him.

'I can't stand it!' the Greek said, touching the tie. 'That and the suit!'

Georgiades was normally a street man and Owen had had his doubts about whether he was up to playing this kind of part. He had, however, the useful gift of looking ordinary in almost any setting and the sympathetic brown eyes invited confidences.

'The suit looks just right,' Owen said.

'You think so?' The Greek looked pleased but wiggled his shoulders uncomfortably. 'Rosa chose it,' he said.

'She did a good job.'

'It cost four,' Georgiades said. 'That's more than you said, but Rosa said the cheaper ones didn't look right.'

'That's fine.'

Four pounds wasn't excessive, and the Greek might have to wear it for some time yet. 'How did you manage?' he asked curiously. 'The talking bit?'

'Oh, fine, fine.'

'I listened to you. I am impressed. Cotton futures!'

'That's Rosa too,' said Georgiades. 'She reads that sort of stuff every day, you know, and told me what to say.'

'Still—'

'The first day or two I just looked at the financial pages of the newspaper and said 'Christ!' from time to time. That seemed to satisfy everybody. It's what they all do, you know. But I hope to God they know more about it than I do!'

'Anyone approached you yet?'

'Not so far.'

Owen sat thinking. He wondered how long he could let this continue. There were costs to this. It was all right if you were getting somewhere, but—

'I think there's a possibility,' said Georgiades, perhaps guessing what Owen was thinking. 'There's someone who might be working up to it. Every day he sort of gets closer. On the verge.'

'All right, then,' said Owen reluctantly. 'We'll carry on for a bit.'

Georgiades nodded.

'You know,' he said, 'I'm getting to quite like this. You sit there every day and people buy you drinks. And it's amazing what you hear! Did you know they're opening some new bases on the Canal? It's not come out yet but these people know it already. I tell you, you can't keep a thing quiet in Egypt. There are spies everywhere!'

The wounded were beginning to arrive from Gallipoli and the hospitals were filling up. There was suddenly a shortage of nurses, and the ladies of the British community volunteered their services enthusiastically. Mrs Cunningham began to draw up lists. Cairns-Grant, however, was less enthusiastic. 'I don't mind the ladies,' he said to Owen, 'but I don't want Mrs Cunningham in every day telling me what to do.'

He had asked Owen to come in and see him because he had another problem to do with nursing on his hands. For many years a not inconsiderable part of the nursing at the hospital had been done by German nuns, but could that now continue? There were many who felt that the nuns should be interned, just as all the other German nationals had been. Owen, who had had to do the interning, was less keen. What possible threat was posed by a community of nuns, he asked? But what about the information they might glean from the soldiers in the wards? Glean, and pass on. Yes, it was spies again. Owen appealed to the Minister, and

Yasin Effendi, without even a glance at the Adviser, deemed that the nuns could remain where they were.

But did that mean that they should continue with their nursing? How could it be expected, in the circumstances, that they should nurse with the devotion of English nurses? Mrs Cunningham's ladies were ready to step into the breach.

'Ay, but the nuns know what they're doing,' said Cairns-Grant.

At his request, Owen had a word with Paul, who had a word with MacMahon, and a compromise was reached whereby the nuns would continue with their duties while the nursing effort generally would be reinforced by Mrs Cunningham's volunteers.

'And ye can tell that auld biddie,' said Cairns-Grant, 'that if there's one bad word to any of my German lassies, then the whole lot of them will be out of the hospital the next day!'

Owen had no intention of telling Mrs Cunningham anything just at the moment because he had his own problem in the nursing sphere. When he had gone home one day he had found Zeinab spitting fire. When she had heard that an auxiliary nursing effort was being organised she had approached Mrs Cunningham to volunteer her services. 'Certainly, my dear,' said Mrs Cunningham. 'I'll put your name down,' But then she heard nothing more.

'And I know what that means,' said Zeinab.

'Forget about Mrs Cunningham,' said Owen. 'Go straight to Cairns-Grant.'

'I don't have to plead to foreigners to be allowed to work in the hospitals of my own country,' raged Zeinab. 'If the British don't want me, I'll nurse Germans.'

Unfortunately, there weren't as yet Germans to nurse, so Zeinab nursed her wrath instead and Owen sharpened his dagger and awaited his opportunity.

ↄﾟﾟﾟↄ

Nikos looked up.

'You remember Sabri?' he said. 'The one who was killed at the Camel Market?'

Owen stopped.

'Yes. You were going to have a word with his family?'

'I've had a word. That's all sorted out. If you'll sign the order, I'll see that a payment goes through every month.'

'Good.'

'But you might like to have a word with them yourself,' said Nikos. 'They said that when he died, Sabri was trying to get a message to you.'

Chapter Three

Sabri came from a village a few miles up river and the next morning Owen borrowed a horse from the Police Barracks and rode out to it.

The village lay a little inland from the Nile, a few white, mud-brick houses beneath some lebbek trees. At the far end was a tall dove-cot which held the villagers' pigeons. From inside came a steady purring. There were pigeons in the lebbek trees, too. They were an important source of meat for the villagers, and also a source of tension. The birds were always raiding the fields nearby, and the few large independent farmers, and the local pasha, who owned most of the land, objected strongly.

The houses were all single-storey. The smaller ones consisted just of two rooms, one in which the family lived, the other which they shared with the family buffalo. The larger ones had, perhaps, an extra room and were surrounded by a wall to form a kind of courtyard in which the children could play and where the women would cook the meals. The flat roofs of all of them were piled high with onions drying in the sun, dates and beans. A few had heaps of brushwood but wood was scarce and most villagers relied for fuel on paraffin or on dried buffalo droppings.

Sabri's house was somewhere in between. It had only two rooms but had a wall around it. The second room, however, was not shared with a buffalo. Sabri had no buffalo. He did not work his land but let it out to a cousin. He rode instead with the Bedawin and their camel herds. He always wanted to be different, his wife told Owen, and he kept himself to himself. That, perhaps, was the meaning of the outer wall.

Sabri's wife received Owen boldly in the courtyard. That was another difference between Sabri and the other villagers. Women usually kept themselves aloof and if they had to talk to a stranger would talk to him only in the presence of a male relative. Owen had been prepared to wait for the cousin but Sabri's wife said that was not necessary.

'I join in your grief,' Owen said.

The woman inclined her head in acknowledgement.

'When a good man goes,' she said, 'the loss goes wider than the household.'

'Your husband served me well,' said Owen, 'and you will stay under my protection.'

'That may be useful,' said the woman, 'for the Pasha Ismail will want our land.'

'Is the land yours or is it rented?' asked Owen.

'It is rented from Al-Fuli,' said the woman, 'but it has been worked by Sabri's family for generations. His father worked it and his grandfather. And they say his father before that. But when it came to his turn Sabri would have none of it. He said if you worked the land, you worked for the pasha. So he let the land out to his cousin and went with the Bedawin.'

'The cousin will surely wish to continue. So why should not Al-Fuli continue to let the land to the people of Sabri?'

'Because the Pasha is greedy for land,' said the woman bitterly. 'He presses whenever there is an opportunity.'

'The money that will come from me,' said Owen, 'is little, but it will be enough for you and your children not to have to depend on the land.'

'The money is welcome,' said the woman. 'But what when I die? Money dries up but land never does.' She turned her head. 'Salah!' she called.

Owen had seen the small boy peering round the corner of the door. Now he came out into the courtyard.

'This is Salah,' said the woman. 'Sabri's son. What will there be for him if the land is taken? Although, God knows, Sabri would never have wanted him to work on the land. "He who works the land is a slave," he said, "and I do not want my son to grow up to be a slave."'

'What, then, did Sabri want for his son?' asked Owen.

The woman was silent for a moment. Then she shrugged.

'He spoke of him riding with him and learning to herd the camels. Or of working for the Government.' She looked at Owen. 'He thought you might help.'

'And so I will. Bring the lad to me when he is old enough.'

'Ah, yes,' said the woman, 'but I am not sure I myself would have it so. Those who work for you do not always die in their beds.'

'There is other work for the Government besides mine. And some of those who work for the Government grow fat and sleek.'

The woman laughed.

'That is true,' she agreed.

'Mother, I would wish to do as my father did,' said the boy.

'And not all who serve me die as your husband did,' said Owen. 'But did your husband die as he did because of his work for me? If he did, then that grieves me and concerns me deeply. But is that so? Did he not die because of some other reason? A quarrel, perhaps?'

'Sabri did not quarrel,' said the woman definitely. 'He would stand up for himself and his own but would let the rest pass. "There is enough foolishness in the world," he said, "without adding to it."'

'But, you see,' said Owen, 'a quarrel might have been put upon him, not of his seeking but one that he could not refuse.'

'If it had,' said the woman bitterly, 'he would not have been found as he was, stuffed like a sheep in the corner of the fiki's booth. He would have borne it out in the open where all could see and bear testimony to the kind of man he was.'

'Well, we shall see,' said Owen. 'The thing must be looked into. For if his death came as the result of a private quarrel, then as a man I grieve for Sabri as a man, but that is an end of it. But if he died because of his work for me, then it is not his quarrel but mine, and by no means at an end.'

A shadow passed over the woman's face.

'These things never have an end,' she said quietly, looking at her son.

'There was word of a message for me,' said Owen.

'As to that,' said the woman, 'you must ask the men. That is men's stuff; and very foolish stuff it seems to be, too.'

༄

Owen went first, as a matter of courtesy, to the cousin, although Sabri's wife had said it would be useless. He was working in the fields.

Close to, the fields were more like allotments than fields, narrow strips, planted with durra, the maize-like crop which was the staple food of the ordinary Egyptian, or else with clover. The strip the cousin was working on was bare and he was ploughing it for the second crop, pulling the plough himself with a harness strapped to his shoulders.

'That is a buffalo's work, not a man's,' said Owen.

'If there is no buffalo, then the man must do it,' said the cousin, not stopping.

Owen fell in beside him.

'You are Sabri's cousin?'

'That is so.'

'I grieve for Sabri.'

The man grunted but did not raise his eyes from the line he was following.

Owen waited a little and then said:

'When a man has to pull the plough himself, there can be little money in the house. And a funeral can be a heavy burden.'

'We have had to go to Al-Fuli again,' said the man bitterly.

'You can repay him. Sabri did work for me from time to time and I will pay for the funeral.'

The cousin turned at the end of the strip and began to walk back. He gave no sign of having heard. When he reached the other end, he said:

'It is a pity Sabri worked for you.'

'Perhaps.'

'I have a wife and children of my own.'

'You will not have to support Sabri's family as well. I will give money for them.'

'Money!' said the man, and laughed bitterly.

Owen continued to walk beside him.

'Our family has always worked this land. My father and his. And theirs. It takes two to work it. Now I will have to work it alone.'

'Has that not been so for some time?'

For the first time, the man looked at him: a quick, surprised look.

'Yes,' he said, 'it has!' He gave a little, angry laugh. 'Even when he was alive, he did little!'

'On the land, perhaps. But did he not bring in money from elsewhere?'

'Little enough. What is camel herding?'

'I gave him money too.'

'Would you had not!' said the man angrily. 'Then Sabri might have been alive today.'

He had not once paused in his ploughing. The sweat was running down his face and over his shoulders.

'What is it you want?' he said.

'Sabri had a message for me.'

'I know nothing of Sabri's messages,' the cousin said, and walked on, his face bent to the ground.

⁂

Sabri's wife had given Owen the name of one of his friends and when Owen got to his house he found him sitting in the courtyard with a group of men drinking tea. One of the men gave a surprised exclamation and jumped up.

'Effendi! You are most welcome here. Do you not know me? It is I, Ibrahim. You spoke for me in the Camel Market.'

'I remember you.'

It was the man on whose behalf he had intervened.

'But I did not know you lived here.'

'This is my village, Effendi, and these my friends.'

'Will you not join us, Effendi?' said one of the men courteously, an older man, whom Owen guessed to be Sabri's friend.

They made room for him and he joined them squatting on the ground. The host went into the house and shortly afterwards a woman came out with a cup, which she placed, eyes lowered, in front of Owen. One of the men poured him tea, the bitter, black tea of the fellahin.

'Do you not remember me, too, Effendi?' asked another of the men.

'I do.'

It was the donkey-barber.

'But what brings you here?' asked Owen. 'Surely not Ibrahim's donkey?'

'If the mountain will not come to Mohammed, Mohammed must go to the mountain,' said the barber, smiling. 'But it is not just for Ibrahim's sake that I come. The fact is, donkeys are getting hard to find these days, now that the Army is taking them all.'

'You'll just have to follow the Army, Anji,' said someone. 'If you are Mohammed, then you've come to the wrong place. The mountain has moved over towards the Canal.'

'Maybe that's what I shall have to do. The trouble is, I'm afraid that when the Turks burst across—' 'when,' Owen noticed—'they may seize me!'

'I am not sure, Anji,' said someone drily, 'that you will be the first that they will seize.'

They all laughed.

'It is true, though, that it is becoming a world without donkeys,' said Owen. 'And without buffalo, too. I saw a man pulling the plough himself.'

'Ah, yes, Ahmed.'

'Sabri's cousin.'

'Ah, yes.'

'I spoke to him. Sabri did some work for me once. I said I would pay towards his funeral. But I am not sure that he heard me.'

The men looked at the ground. He sensed a certain awkwardness.

'Ahmed is not himself, Effendi,' said someone.

'Grief is understandable.'

'It is not just that, Effendi,' said someone quietly.

'No?'

'He is ashamed, Effendi,' said someone, after a moment.

'Why so?'

The man hesitated.

'He has not resented the injury,' he said reluctantly.

'How could he? The killer is not known.'

'I do not know, Effendi. But—but he should have done more. He is the man of the household. He should have gone to the Bedawin and said: "You owe our family a blood debt."'

'But he would not, Effendi,' said another man. 'He is not... not that kind of man.'

'He has a wife and family,' said Owen.

'Yes.'

'And then there are Sabri's wife and children, too, to be looked after.'

'Yes. But—'

'It wasn't the Bedawin, anyway,' said the donkey-barber. 'They would not have denied it.'

'It must have been someone. He should have asked. He should have taken it upon himself, not left it to the boy.'

And now Owen understood the shadow that had passed over the face of Sabri's wife. The honour code was still a force to be reckoned with in Egypt, especially outside the towns. It was the duty of the male member of a family to avenge any affront or injury to the family. Not to do so was to expose oneself and one's family to disgrace.

'It bites deep into Ahmed, Effendi,' said someone, in explanation, not extenuation.

And if no one else took on the duty of revenge, it passed to
the dead man's son. When the boy grew up he would kill and
probably be killed. These things, as Sabri's wife had said, never
had an end.

'This concerns me,' said Owen. He had been wondering how
he could broach the matter and now he thought he could see a
way. 'It concerns me deeply. I do not know how Sabri died or
why he died. But from time to time he did work for me. Suppose a quarrel were put upon him on my behalf? Arising out of
the work he did for me. Then it is I who must avenge it. Not
Sabri's cousin, nor Sabri's son.'

'That is true, Effendi.'

There were general nods of agreement.

'But is it so? Did Sabri die in some way because of me? I ask,
not knowing the answer. The matter is dark to me. I ask your
counsel.'

He could see that they were thinking it over.

'I would not wish to evade my responsibilities.'

'No, no!'

'Of course not!'

'We can see that.'

'On the other hand, these are not duties that should be taken
on lightly.'

'Quite right.'

'I need to be sure that they are mine. And so I come to you,
as men who knew Sabri: there was not some other quarrel that
he was party to? Perhaps in the village?'

'Oh no. Nothing like that.'

'No, no.'

'Sabri was not a quarrelling man.'

'He bore himself easily.'

'Nothing in the village, then? No one?'

'No. Nothing like that.'

'In the city, perhaps?'

'How could it be? He was hardly ever there.'

'That's why I think it was something to do with the Bedawin.'

That seemed to be the general feeling.

'That could well be,' said Owen. 'But I just wanted to be sure before going among them. For they are hot-tempered and rash, and quick to fancy an insult where there is none.'

'Well, that is true.'

'It's best to be careful, with that lot.'

'I just wanted to be sure. You see, there was something that made me wonder a bit.'

'Yes?'

'There was word that Sabri had a message for me. I wondered if that could be anything to do with it. You know, if perhaps he'd got into a fight on my behalf, and wanted to warn me, lest I be come upon unexpectedly—'

'No, no,' said Sabri's friend, 'that wasn't anything to do with it.'

'You know about the message?'

'Yes. He told me about it. It came about thus.

'After he had returned with the Bedawin and delivered the camels to the Camel Market, he came home to his wife. And she was glad to see him after so long. But on the next day she said to him: "Your return is timely, for Al-Fuli has been round here asking for the rent."

'But Sabri said: "It is not so timely, for I have already spent half my earnings." And his wife upbraided him and said: "How can this be? Surely you know of the need for the rent? Now Al-Fuli will take our land from us." But Sabri said: "Some things are more important than land." But she continued to upbraid him and cried: "What things are more important than a living for your family, you foolish man?" For she thought he had misspent the money.'

Sabri's friend paused and looked at Owen.

'But he had not, Effendi. I know what he had done with it. For he came round to see me and told me. He had put aside money for his son to go to the madrissa.'

'Surely it is not necessary to do that?' said Owen. Schools were free in Egypt.

'He wanted him to go to the best madrissa. And for that, extra is necessary. He had spoken of it to me often. "My boy shall not be a slave of the land," he said. "He is clever, and should not be cut off from the things that should be his." So every time he returned, he went to one of the great banks in the City and put aside part of his earnings.'

He broke off and looked at Owen again, with sharp, intelligent eyes.

'Normally, Effendi, I would agree with him, for it is good to think ahead for one's children. But this time I said, "Is it wise, Sabri, to have money in the bank and yet be thrown off one's land because one cannot pay the rent?"

'But Sabri said: "We will not be thrown off our land, for I will be able to pay the rent," It was then, Effendi, that he told me. "I have something to tell the Mamur Zapt," he said. "I go to the Camel Market this evening, and when I tell him tomorrow, he will reward me richly. Let Al-Fuli wait but a little and there will be no question of his not being paid." So you see, Effendi, it was not as you supposed. He wished to see you not because of some quarrel that had come upon you both but because of some mighty thing that he wished to tell you.'

'You have no idea what that thing was?'

'Alas, no, Effendi. I know only that it was something for which he thought you would reward him richly, and that it was something for your ear alone.'

꧁꧂

When Owen left the house he found two men waiting outside. One was a short, stocky, middle-aged man, not an Arab, Turkish-Egyptian, probably, dressed in European clothes. The other was an elderly fellah, grey-haired and dressed in a galabeah.

The one in European clothes came forward, hand outstretched.

'Osman Huq,' he said. 'I am the Pasha Ismail's agent.'

'Owen. Police.'

'Police?'

'A man has been killed. He came, I understand, from this village.'

'Ah, yes. Sabri.' He seemed puzzled, however. 'Police?' he said again.

In Egypt responsibility for investigating a crime lay not with the Police but with the Parquet, the Department of Prosecutions of the Ministry of Justice.

'I am assisting the Parquet in this case.'

'Ah, yes. There is something…special about it?'

'Only that Sabri was helping to supply camels to the Army at the time. We wouldn't want anything to go wrong with the supplying.'

'No, of course not.'

'Nor with the supplying of donkeys. You have been having difficulties, I gather?' he said to the other man, guessing that he was the village omda, or headman.

They shook hands.

'Not really, Effendi. Some have murmured, it is true, but the price was a fair one.'

'There are always people who murmur,' said the agent.

'It affects their ability to work the land, of course.'

'Only a little. There are still donkeys in the village and they can be shared. Besides, there are still buffalo. No, Effendi, it is just that there are always people who are difficult.'

'And that is true,' said the omda.

Osman Huq hesitated.

'Effendi, I am surprised that you should bother yourself with one such as Sabri.'

'Well, I am not bothering myself very much.'

'No, Effendi, I should think not!'

'Sabri was a difficult man if ever there was one,' said the omda.

'He was one who murmured,' said the steward, nodding his head significantly.

'A trouble-maker, was he?'

'Yes!' said the omda.

'He was away most of the time,' said the agent, 'but when he was back there was always something.'

'He didn't know his place,' said the omda.

'Place?' said Owen.

'Well, the people here have always worked for the Pasha Ismail,' said the agent. 'Either directly or indirectly. On his land or, nowadays, on their own, but selling their crops through him. Mostly it's cotton, but not so much,' he looked around, 'round here. But Sabri wasn't content with that.'

'His father was content, and his grandfather,' said the omda. 'So what was so special about Sabri?'

'Will you be staying in the village long, Effendi?' asked Osman Huq.

'No, I go now.'

They shook hands.

'There is nothing for me in this,' said Owen. 'Take care, however, that it does not turn into honour killings.'

'We will, Effendi, never fear,' said the Pasha's agent. 'Sabri's death ends here.'

Chapter Four

'Well done, Owen!' said Curtis.

'Thank you,' said Owen, mystified.

He collected his whisky and headed off through the crowd at the bar.

'Good work, Owen,' said Cunningham. 'One by one!'

There were approving pats as he moved through the throng.

'Great stuff, Owen!' said someone, giving him the "thumbs-up" signal. 'One down, only a thousand to go!'

'Excellent!' said Cavendish, touching him on the shoulder. 'Just what we need!'

'Congratulations, Gareth!' said Paul Trevelyan, raising a glass.

'What the hell is all this?' demanded Owen, sitting down opposite him.

'Your latest triumph.'

'What *is* my latest triumph?'

Paul stared at him.

'You don't know?'

'I haven't been back to my office today.'

'Well, in your absence, things have been moving. Your people have caught a spy.'

The Australian officer he'd seen talking to Maxwell was sitting next to Paul.

'You really don't know?' he said. 'Well, that's the mark of a good office, I suppose. The people who do the work get on with it without bothering to tell the boss.'

'It comes at just the right time, too,' said Paul. 'People were beginning to get a thing about spies.'

'Spies everywhere,' said the Australian, 'and the moment you turn round, the bastards have all gone.'

'It will show we're on top of things,' said Paul, toasting Owen again.

'Er, yes,' said Owen. 'Well, yes.'

'Down in the cells,' said Nikos, without looking up.

There were some cells at the Bab el Khalk but the Mamur Zapt himself rarely had occasion to use them. For the most part they were used by the regular police. It was, in fact, two regular policemen, swelling with pride, who had been responsible for the arrest.

'Suspect was observed attempting to suborn a guard at the Abdin Palace. Suspect then offered the guard seditious literature. The guard took it at first, thinking it was pornographic but then, realising his mistake, handed it back. Suspect then attempted to suborn two more guards. One of them kept the literature, Effendi, which is available for submission as evidence. Suspect then invited him to a meeting. Guard replied—what did the guard reply, Abou?'

'Any time, darling.'

'Any time, darling?'

'Officer then went to the place assigned for the meeting. It was found to be a cellar occupied by a low printing press. Officer waited until the guard came and then asked what guard was doing there. Guard replied—what did guard reply, Abou?'

'Just looking for a copy of *The Times*.'

'Officers arrested guard for being a cheeky bastard. Guard then confessed all. His evidence will form the basis of—'

'Yes, yes. But what's all this about spying?'

'Suspect endeavoured to obtain information from the guards, Effendi.'

'What sort of information?'

'When they were coming off duty. Would they like to come to a meeting—'

'Yes, yes, I've got that bit. But—'

'Wait, Effendi. This is the real clincher. Suspect then asked guard if he knew when he would be going to the front. Guard replied—what did the guard reply, Abou?'

'Never, if he could bloody help it.'

'Thank you, Abou. Suspect said that was the right attitude. Why should Egyptian soldiers fire on their brothers? Suspect asked guard, what about him personally? Would he be willing to open fire on his brothers across the Canal? Guard replied—what did guard—?'

'He said it wasn't that that bothered him. What bothered him was that they might open fire on him.'

'Thank you, Abou. Suspect then said that he should turn his gun on the real enemy, who were back at home.'

'Yes, that certainly seems very questionable, but—'

'And, finally, Effendi—'

'Yes?'

'Suspect said: "They're building some new camps in the Canal. Tell us when you're going, and if you can find out anything about them"…Yes, Abou?'

'Hot as hell.'

'Yes, well, thank you, Abou. Well, that's about it, Effendi. The guard is prepared to testify, although he says he'd prefer not to. We've got the seditious material…Yes, Abou? Oh, yes. Arrest. Suspect came to the printing shop. Suspect was observed to pick up a pile of leaflets and then take them to her school, where she—'

'She?' said Owen. 'School?'

She was, Owen judged—although judging was difficult because of the veil which covered her mouth and nose and concealed her hair—about fifteen.

'What is your name?' he asked.

'Yasmin,' said the girl sulkily.

'The rest of it.'

She shook her head determinedly.

'You are still at school?'

After a moment she nodded.

'Which school?' And then, as she began to shake her head again: 'You might as well tell me. You were seen there, after all, by the officer arresting you.'

'The Sanieh,' she said unwillingly.

It was one of the best schools in Cairo; *the* best girls' school.

'They shouldn't have arrested me,' she said. 'I wasn't committing an offence.'

'Well, you were, I'm afraid. You were distributing seditious material in the playground. And you had previously tried to give it to the guards at the Abdin Palace.'

'I do not regard that as an offence.'

'The law does, I'm afraid. The leaflets you were distributing are classified as seditious literature and banned by the Government. And distributing them is an offence.'

'I do not recognise a law made by the British.'

'This one wasn't.'

'I do not recognise the Sultan, either. Not this one. He is just a puppet of the British. And the Assembly, too. They're all puppets.'

'Nevertheless, you have committed an offence.'

She was silent for a moment. Then her eyes flashed.

'All right, then,' she said, holding out her hands as if for handcuffs, 'charge me! Go on, charge me! Bring me to trial. I demand to be brought to trial. Then all the world will see how the British treat Egyptians. I *want* you to bring me to trial.'

'Hold on. It can't be done as quickly as that. You're a minor, and—'

She glared at him.

'I demand that you put me on trial!' she said, stamping her foot. 'I shall not deny anything, anything that stupid guard says, or the even more stupid police. I do not deny it, but nor do I acknowledge any guilt. I deny the Court's legitimacy. And that is what I shall say in Court. "You have no right," I shall say. "You have no right to try me. I deny your legitimacy. You are puppets of the British. Sentence me if you dare! I am not afraid. Send me to prison if you wish, but Egypt will fight on. You cannot send the whole of Egypt to prison." Yes, that is what I shall say: "You cannot send us all to prison!"'

'Yes, well. Very fine. However, I doubt if it will come to that.'

'But I *want* it to come to that!' she said fiercely.

'I daresay, but it's not as easy as that. For a start, you're still at school—'

'I won't be for long. Not when the Headmistress finds out.'

'And this is a first offence.'

'I shall repeat it,' she said. 'Believe me!'

'Besides, it is a very minor offence. Although, admittedly if they decided to press the subornment charge—'

'"Suborn"?' she said. 'What is that?'

'Inducing someone to commit an illegal action.'

'I don't think I've done that, have I?' she said doubtfully. More firmly: 'Yet.'

'Well, it could be argued that by trying to persuade the soldier not to fire on the enemy— But, frankly, I don't think that would be enough to get yourself sent to prison. Not in the circumstances.'

The girl considered.

'What about that information that you were trying to get out of the guard?' asked Owen. 'I think that might be your best bet.'

'Information?'

'You know, about the camps on the Canal.'

'I wasn't really—'

'If you had got it, who would you have passed it on to?'

'I'm not sure. But I would soon have found somebody.'

Owen shook his head.

'It won't do, I'm afraid. I'm afraid that all they'll do is let you off with a caution.'

'But I don't *want* to be let off!'

'Sorry.'

'If you do not try me and send me to prison,' said Yasmin passionately, 'I shall go straight back and distribute some more leaflets. No!' The eyes above the veil lit up. 'I know what I shall do. I will go and chain myself to the railings of the Palace. Just as the women in England do!'

6~~9

The fiki's booth was not in the Camel Market proper as that might have been seen by some as discrepant with his function, which was intoning passages from the Holy Writing for the benefit of passers-by. While animals would certainly benefit too, they could not benefit as much as those with greater understanding. More to the point, they might not receive the words with the respect that was their due.

The booth had therefore been situated not in that part of the Market where the animals were kept and displayed but among the more general stalls outside. It consisted of three walls of embroidered carpeting, each about six feet long and five feet high, together with a fourth side which was rather taller and bent over at the top in a kind of canopy beneath which the fiki could sit in the shade. Sabri's body had been stuffed behind the carpeting of the fourth side. There were some extra folds there which had made it easier. Given that people in Egypt had learned never to look behind things, the body might have lain there for some time undisturbed among the excrement had it not been for the small boys of the Market; although, as he pointed out to Owen, the fiki himself would surely have detected the presence before long.

The small boys, creeping round the booth in the early morning while the fiki was yet sleeping, had seen a hand protruding from the folds. At first they had taken it to be the fiki's and had contemplated placing a small scorpion in the palm. Then, however, they had realised that the snoring was coming from another part of the booth. They had deliberated for some time whether the hand belonged to a Bedawin or a beggar and had tried tickling it with a feather. Eventually they had convinced themselves that they had found a genuine body.

They had awoken the fiki and alerted first the neighbours and then, as they reminded him, Owen. Owen's lack of interest on that earlier occasion was made up for now. They showed him where they had seen the hand and how exactly the body had lain: adding vivid but less plausible details as to the appearance of the body when at last the Effendi from the Parquet had come and ordered it to be slung across a camel and be taken away.

Owen stood for some time looking down on the place where Sabri had lain. There were smears of blood on the carpeting. He could not see any, however, on the sand around. Sabri must have been killed elsewhere, probably nearby, and the body brought. There should have been traces. The sand was all scuffed up by now so perhaps it was not surprising that he couldn't see them. But the sand would have been less disturbed when the Parquet man had come and he would certainly have looked. It would be in his report. Had he called in trackers, Owen wondered?

The body had been found in the morning. This meant it had been placed there during the night. Where had Sabri been that night?

His nose caught a whiff of smoke from a dung fire. He looked across the Camel Market to where the Bedawin were preparing their evening meal. That would probably have been where.

He walked over to one of the fires. They made room for him with the casual hospitality of the nomad. One of them put a cup of tea into his hands. He sat there for some time, getting used to their Arabic, a different Arabic from that used in the city and the one that he was familiar with.

'You will be leaving soon?' he said eventually.

'Tomorrow.'

Owen nodded and sipped his tea.

'One of you will not be leaving,' he said, after a moment.

'No?'

'The one who was killed.'

'True.'

'Not one of you,' Owen said.

'No,' they agreed.

'Although he rode with you. Compensation must be paid. And his people need to know who it is that must pay it.'

'Not us,' they said.

'He was with you,' Owen pointed out.

They shrugged.

'Was there not some quarrel?'

'No,' they said.

'Some cause of strife?'

'How could there be? He was not one of our enemies. He came from round here.'

'They don't have tribes in the city,' one of them explained.

The most usual cause of trouble among the Bedawin was a tribal feud.

'Some private things?' he suggested. 'Hot words?'

They looked at each other and shook their heads.

'He kept himself to himself and bore himself modestly.'

'Nevertheless, on a long journey—?'

He could see, however, that they dismissed it.

'Why do you ask?' said one of the Bedawin suspiciously. 'Are you charging us with his death?'

'No. It is just that since he was with you, you might know who his family should apply to for compensation.'

'If it was us,' said the man truculently, 'do you not think we would have said?'

'I know that you, being the men you are, would not deny a just quarrel.'

'If there had been a quarrel with one of us,' persisted the man, 'it would have been out in the open. We do not creep up upon a man in the night.'

There were mutters of agreement from all round the fire. The Bedawin regarded the point as conclusive.

'I do not charge you with his death. I seek only your help. And surely I can seek it, since, although he was not one of you, he rode with you?'

They considered this carefully. The Bedawin system of obligations, although stringent, made neat discriminations.

'I ask on behalf of the family of one who rode with you.'
They looked at each other.
'I ask only for your help.'
'Well—'
He could see they were weakening.
'There are bad men around,' said someone.
'It's like that in the city,' said someone else.
'And you think it was one of them?'
'Must have been.'
'To come upon a man in the dark!'
'When he was just doing his job!'
'Ah, he was doing his job, was he? I thought he had finished and gone home.'
'He had. But then he came back. Just for the night.'
'Why was that?'
'He said he had to see someone the next morning.'
'Could he not have come the next day? Why should he spend the night with you?'
'He said it was to see a big man, Effendi.' It was 'Effendi' now, Owen noticed. 'At one of the Government offices. You can spend all day there waiting to see someone like that. He thought he'd better get there early.'
'And so he spent the night with you?'
'That's right, Effendi,' said someone who had not yet spoken. 'He was with Wajja and me at our fire.'
'Then how was it that he was taken?'
'The camels were restless. And Wajja said: "We must go and look, for there may be thieves abroad: and if someone takes the camels, maybe the Levantine will want his money back." So Sabri said: "I will go, for I have been too near the fire, and must cool off."'
'And he went?'
'That is so.'
'And then?'
'Then? Nothing. He did not come back. And I would have been content to leave it so, but Wajja—'

'I said I was uneasy. For the camels were still restless. So I took my sword and my whip and went among them. But I found nothing untoward and no person there, not even Sabri. So after a while I went back to the fire and found Mukhtar sleeping, and woke him up and told him.'

'And he said: "Thank you very much, Wajja. The next time you find nothing, perhaps you will tell someone else? Sabri has doubtless gone to find some woman and it is no business of ours." But the next morning the small boys of the Market came and taunted us from afar, crying: "What manner of men are you, that allow yourselves to be taken sleeping?"'

☙

Owen had heard the distant clanging of a bell in the night but it was sufficiently far away to be of no immediate concern and he had turned over and gone back to sleep. The next morning he had forgotten about it but it came back to him when, towards noon, McPhee stuck his head in at the door and said:

'Owen, I wonder if you would mind coming along to my office? This is something for you, I think, rather than for me.'

In McPhee's office he found a representative from the Mufti, Cairo's religious leader, and a smooth young man from the Khedive's—no, not the Khedive's now, he would never get used to this new style, the Sultan's—Office.

'What's the trouble?'

'The Mufti wishes to register his concern.'

'And so does His Royal Highness.'

'Oh, yes. What about?'

'The Australians,' said McPhee glumly.

'Their behaviour,' said the man from the Sultan's Office.

'I'm sorry to hear that. In what respect?'

'Their drinking. And its consequences.'

'There was a fire last night,' said McPhee.

It was then that Owen remembered the bell.

'Oh, dear. No one hurt, I hope?'

'There would have been,' said the Mufti's representative, 'but for the grace of God.'

'A liquor house was set on fire,' said McPhee.

'Another one? There was one the other day.'

'That's right.'

'And you think it was the Australians?'

'They were the only ones in it,' the man from the Sultan's Office pointed out.

'Muslims don't drink alcohol,' said the Mufti's representative.

'I'm afraid some of them do.'

'It is disapproved of by the Prophet.'

'Of course. The Australians, I'm afraid, are ignorant of this.'

'Could they not be reminded?'

'I will try.' Honesty compelled him to add: 'I don't know how much effect it will have, however. They come from a country where alcohol is not disapproved of.'

'But they are in another country now.'

'That is true; and perhaps they should have more respect for its customs.'

'The problem is, liquor houses are springing up everywhere,' said McPhee.

'Cannot you do something about this?' asked the man from the Sultan's Office.

'I could, of course, restrict the number granted licences. But that would merely drive their customers into the unlicensed ones.'

'If they're unlicensed, you should close them down.'

'I try to. The difficulty is—'

They all knew what the difficulty was. It was the capitulations, a system of legal privileges which over the years the Egyptians had been obliged to grant to foreigners. They restricted, for example, the authorities' right of access to premises owned by foreigners; so that when Owen arrived and demanded entry, he could be denied it until he returned with a Consular representative of the country the owner of the premises claimed to belong to. And when he *did* return with the Consular representative, he found more often than not that meanwhile the nationality claimed by the owner had changed. It was so frustrating for the police that in the end they usually preferred not to bother.

'The trouble is,' said McPhee, 'that there are safety implications.'

'The risk of fire, you mean, like this one?'

'They go up in flames. It's the spirit.'

'It is not right,' said the Mufti's representative, 'that the lives and property of ordinary Egyptians should be put at risk because of the habits of foreign soldiers—'

'Stationed on our soil against our will!'

'They are defending the country, of course,' said Owen. 'However, let us not go into that. What we are all agreed on is that something must be done about the fire.'

'And the drinking,' said the Mufti's representative.

'Certainly: if we can.'

'The two go together.'

'The three go together,' said the man from the Sultan's Office. 'There wasn't a problem before the Australians came.'

'Well, I don't know that I quite agree with you there,' said Owen. 'The consumption of alcohol was not exactly unknown in Egypt before the Australians came. And, anyway, are we sure that they alone are to be blamed for the fire?'

Chapter Five

'It would be a pity,' said Georgiades, settling back in the soft chair and sipping his gin-and-tonic.

'Yes, well I can't afford to have you going on like this. There are other jobs I need you on.'

'Like what?'

'Well, there's a fire that needs investigating.'

'Fire,' said Georgiades unenthusiastically.

'Yes. I need you on the streets.'

Georgiades swirled the ice at the bottom of his glass and signalled to the waiter for another one.

'It would be a pity,' he said. 'Just when I'm getting somewhere here.'

'Oh, yes?'

'Yes. Really getting somewhere.'

'You said that last time.'

'On the verge, I think I said. And now it's really beginning to happen.'

'Oh, yes?' said Owen sceptically.

'Yes. I've had an approach.'

'I think you said that last time, too.'

'I said I was expecting one. And now I've had it.'

'Really had one?'

'Yes. Swiss, I think he is. If I could let him have some cotton, routed, of course, via Stockholm, he thinks he could dispose of it for me. At a price which would surprise me.'

Owen hesitated. He had come determined to get Georgiades back on normal duties. The job was taking too long. It had been wished on him by the authorities in England. Some of Egypt's cotton crop was escaping local controls and being sold in Europe and Owen had been asked to investigate the Egyptian end. Important, no doubt; but was it important enough to justify lying up one of his best agents? Still, if Georgiades was just about to get somewhere—

Georgiades took the glass from the waiter, tasted it and then put it down for the ice to work.

'Mind you,' he continued, 'any price would surprise me. I wouldn't know a good one from a bad one. But Rosa says it's all right.'

'Rosa?'

'Yes. She follows these things, you know. I think she gets it from her grandmother. Her business sense. Her parents certainly haven't got it. Nor me, neither, unfortunately. Anyway, what she says is, accept the other offer—'

'Other offer?'

'Didn't I tell you about that? Sorry. Well, I've had two approaches. One wants to buy from me, the other to sell to me. Rosa says, accept the offer to sell to me—she says the price is right, it's lower than the other one, apparently that's important, Christ, I don't understand these things—and then sell it on to the Swiss. At the price he said.'

'Yes, well, look, I don't know that I wanted you to get as far as actual dealing—'

'That's what I said to her. I'm just there to catch them, I said, not to try and make my bloody fortune. "Make your fortune as well," she said, "on the side. It'll set us up for life." But I don't know. Frankly, this kind of thing terrifies me. Anything to do with money. I give my pay to her each week and let her get on with it. She seems to have an instinct for it. But I reckon it's best if she leaves me out of it. I always get these damned things the wrong way round, you know, think the selling price is the buying price, that sort of thing.'

'Look, never mind the deal, just keep them dangling for a while—'

'Yes, that's what Rosa says. She says the Swiss price will go up and the Egyptian price will go down.'

'Never mind that. If you've got both a potential seller and a potential buyer, we're beginning to get somewhere. Can you let Nikos have the details, so that he can do some background digging? And, meanwhile, I suppose you'd better stay on here—'

'That's what I thought,' said Georgiades, giving the ice in his glass a swirl.

⁊ℳ℘

That afternoon Owen went to the Parquet offices in the Ministry of Justice and asked if he could see their file on Sabri. Caught off-guard, for they were not used to visits from the Mamur Zapt, they could think, on the spur of the moment, of no reason why he shouldn't, so he was taken into a small room and the file laid before him.

There was as yet little in it: the formal notification from the Police of the body's having been found, a note assigning a Parquet officer to the case, together with a signed slip indicating that he had taken up his duties, and an initial medical report recording that the deceased had died of stab wounds inflicted from behind. There was, disappointingly, no account of the Parquet officer's visit to the Camel Market.

He concentrated on the medical report. 'Inflicted from behind.' That made it less likely that Sabri had died in a quarrel. As the result of one, possibly, but not in one. There was, too, no mention of other knife wounds such as would probably have been the case in a knife fight. This was only an initial report and he would have to await the final one, but if there had been other wounds they would probably have been mentioned.

Or perhaps they might not have been. The report was scribbled and showed every sign of having been written in a hurry. He wondered whether to ask Cairns-Grant to take an interest in the case.

The door behind him opened. He had been half-expecting that. The Parquet guarded its territory jealously and although the Mamur Zapt was in principle a colleague, he was one whom the strongly Nationalist Parquet preferred to keep at a distance.

'Can I help you?' said a voice.

It was a slightly nervous young man in the usual dark suit of the Parquet.

'Hassan Marbri,' he said, introducing himself. 'I have been assigned to this case.'

They shook hands.

'Can I help you?' he said again.

'Probably not at the moment. You've only just started, haven't you?'

'You are taking an interest in the case?'

'A limited one.'

The lawyer hesitated.

'May I ask the motive of your interest?'

Owen knew what was worrying him. The Mamur Zapt normally dealt only with cases which had a political dimension.

'It is merely that at the time of his death, the deceased was working for the Government—he was delivering camels to the Army. Supplies just want to be sure that this wasn't a factor in his death.'

'It's hardly likely, is it?'

'Well, I don't know. The requisitioning of domestic animals is highly unpopular in the countryside.'

'Yes, but the camels wouldn't have been requisitioned, would they? They'd have been bought, somewhere over in the west.'

'Almost certainly. This is just a routine check.' If the Parquet guarded its territory, so did Owen, and he didn't think it politic to reveal that Sabri had worked for him. 'However, it has to be made.'

'Quite so.'

The young lawyer seemed relieved.

'By the way,' said Owen, 'there wasn't a report of your visit to the Market. You have made one?'

'Oh, yes,' said Hassan Marbri, 'to pick up the body. It's still in draft,' he said apologetically.

'Did you look around?'

'Of course.'

'Find anything?'

'The body had been hidden beneath the carpeting of a fiki's booth.'

'But he hadn't been killed there. Or had he?'

'There was blood on the carpeting.'

'Anywhere else?'

'Not that I could see. But by the time I got there, the ground had been badly scuffed up. It's a Market, after all.'

'Did you call in the trackers?'

'Trackers?' said the lawyer, looking on him in surprise. 'In the city?'

ᘒᘒᘒ

There was something familiar about the man Nikos showed into the office. Owen was sure he had seen him before but, for the moment, couldn't quite place him.

'Mohammed Sekhmet,' said Nikos.

He was a short, middle-aged man wearing the red tarboosh of the Egyptian *functionnaire*, Government employee, which he took off on entering, in deference to British custom, to reveal close-cropped grey hair. The face wasn't Arab; Turkish, Owen fancied.

'I have come to thank you,' he said, 'for releasing my daughter.'

'Daughter?'

'Yasmin.'

'Oh, yes.' Owen had released Yasmin the day before. 'No thanks are needed,' he said. 'She is young and would be better under the eye of her father.'

Mohammed Sekhmet sighed.

'Do not think she has *not* been under the eye of her father, Effendi. When she goes out, it is always with a servant beside her. Even when she goes to school. But, Effendi, the school is big and there are many gates. Too often, at the end of the day, the servant waits at the appointed gate but she does not come. She has left by another. And then she goes off and does such terrible things!'

'Well, well, the young are often rebellious.'

'Effendi, *I* was not rebellious. I did what my father decreed. But the young these days—there is a different spirit to the age!'

'The world changes.'

'I know, I know. That is what my daughter says when I chide her. She looks on me, I fear, as one that belongs to the past. I cannot get near her.'

'It is a common story.'

'But how will the story end, Effendi? That is what worries me. For once you have set your foot on a path, you have to follow where it leads.'

'We shall have to see that she doesn't go down the path. She is still young, and we must help her to find other paths.'

Mohammed Sekhmet sighed again.

'We have tried, Effendi, her mother and I. We try all the time.'

'Perhaps this will bring it home to her.'

Even as he spoke, Owen, remembering his exchanges with Yasmin, had his doubts.

Mohammed Sekhmet looked at him.

'It has to come to this, Effendi, does it?' he said quietly.

'To the court, you mean? Well, that is what I have to think about. I could, I think, get her let off with a caution, although I would have to speak to the Police and to the Parquet about it. But would she heed the warning?'

Mohammed Sekhmet's face looked wretched.

'I wish I could say that she would, Effendi, but I cannot.'

'Is there someone that she might listen to? At her school, perhaps?'

'Effendi, I have spoken to the headmistress many times about my daughter and I have always found her just and helpful. But now she has to think of the other pupils. One bad date can infect the rest.'

'Has she expelled her?'

'She is thinking of doing so. And I cannot blame her.'

'I will speak with her. Perhaps she may know someone.'

Mohammed Sekhmet bowed his head in acknowledgement and then sat for a while looking down at the floor. Then he raised his eyes.

'Effendi,' he said quietly, 'all my hopes were in her. Her brother is afflicted and the ability is lacking. All he will ever be able to do is work with me at the Fire Brigade.'

And now Owen knew why his face had seemed familiar. He was the senior fireman who had so intelligently diverted the hoses at the fire Owen had witnessed the other day and driven the spectators away to safety.

'If he grows up to be as worthy a man as his father, why should one ask for more?'

Mohammed Sekhmet flushed slightly.

'But in my daughter, Effendi, the ability shines out. My wife said: 'It is time for her to marry.' But I said, no, she has a rare quality that must not be denied. Let her go to the madrissa, and then on to the great madrissa, and then perhaps she will be able to serve those around her as God bids us to do and as her father, imperfectly, has tried to do.'

'Those were wise words.'

'No, Effendi, they were not. They were foolish, vain words. It was presumptuous in me. I aspired too highly for her, and now I am justly punished.'

'No, no, no, no.'

'Yes, Effendi, yes! I thrust her forward, when I should have waited for God to raise her if He thought fit. For God sees into the hearts, and perceives what man does not. He perceived the spirit of rebellion in her which I had made myself blind to.'

'No—'

'Effendi, I and my family have always seen life as service. In my case it was service to the Khedive, in the case of my wife and her family, service to the Pasha. But now my daughter raises her voice against Khedive and Pasha! Where will this end? For the rebellious spirit there is no end, there is just the rebelliousness that goes on and on, tearing down all it meets until it tears apart the world! And that is my daughter, Effendi. Effendi, what shall I do?'

⟨ܘܐܘ⟩

There were two of them, desert men from the Red Sea hills, with short-skirted galabeahs and heavy tribal scars on their faces. They bent down over the place where Sabri's body had been found, almost as if they were dogs sniffing, and stayed there for some time. Then they began to circle out from the spot, their eyes fixed on the ground.

One of them called to the other and they bent down over something. Then they began to move again, this time in a series of zig-zags across an imaginary line leading out from the fiki's booth.

Owen went across and asked what they had found. They showed him two little black drops of congealed blood, black, dung-like specks almost concealed by the sand. Then, a few feet away, they showed him another. And then another, hard, with sand sticking on it, almost like an old sheep's turd.

The line led to that part of the Market where the camels were normally tethered, although there were no camels there now. The drops were bigger now, occasional little bitumen-like dark patches an inch or more across. One of the trackers told him that Sabri's galabeah must have soaked up a lot of the blood.

In the Camel Market proper they nosed about for some time. At last they stood up and beckoned to him. They said that Sabri had died here, among the camels. Perhaps he had come out from among the sleeping Bedawin to still them. He had stood here, beside this tethering stake, for here on the wood were dried brown splashes and, at the base of the stake, a dark pancake gritted with sand, indicating that the body had fallen just about here...

⟨ܘܐܘ⟩

The Australians were holding a Mess Night. At least, that is what it would have been called when the British had occupied the Barracks. The Australians called it a Party and there was something a great deal freer about the occasion than when the Army had entertained Owen before. For a start, women had been positively invited.

'Are you sure?' said Owen. 'It's okay if I bring my wife?'

'You'll be very popular if you do bring your wife. A lot of us have only just landed and won't have seen a woman since we left Australia.'

'But, by God,' said the Commander in Chief gloomily, as he stood next to Owen that evening, looking round on the jollity, 'they'll soon be making up for it. If they're anything like the other Australians. Can't you do something to get them out of the brothels, Bill?' he said to a senior Australian officer standing nearby.'

'No,' said the Australian. 'But don't worry about it. We'll prise them off when the time comes.'

'Yes, but by that time they'll all be down with V.D.'

'That is a problem, I admit.' The incidence of venereal disease was already almost a quarter in some units. 'But they'll be all right when we get them over to the Canal. It's just here in the city that there's a problem. A brothel on every corner and two drinking houses in between. They think it's Paradise.'

'Can't you do something about that, Owen?'

'No.'

'Don't tell me,' said the Australian he'd met before: 'they're all owned by foreigners, right?'

'Right,' said Owen.

'And you can't touch them?'

'Only with difficulty.'

'Well, we're going to have to do something about it,' said the Commander in Chief. 'Couldn't you just put them off limits for troops, Bill?'

'You could,' said the Australian doubtfully.

'Actually, there's something I wanted to talk to you about,' said Owen. He told them about the visit he'd received from the emissaries of the Mufti and the Sultan. They talked about it for a moment or two but couldn't see much that could be done about it.

'Anyway,' said the Australian, 'we'll be out of here soon. Either in Gallipoli or across the Canal.'

Faruq, the Prince who had been at the High Commissioner's reception, came into the room. He looked round and then went straight to Zeinab. She was surrounded by a ring of Australians. They opened up hospitably to let the Prince in. He obviously expected them to go away but they didn't.

'I can't make that bloke out,' said Maxwell, the Commander in Chief. 'Is he for us or against us?'

'We don't know,' said Paul Trevelyan, who had just joined the group. 'But we've got to make sure. The Sultan's getting on a bit and Faruq could be the next in line.'

The Prince was trying to manoeuvre Zeinab out of the ring but, Owen was glad to see, she kept manoeuvring back.

'You're pretty busy at the hospital, I gather?' Maxwell said to Cairns-Grant.

'They keep coming in.'

Everyone knew that the casualties at Gallipoli had been heavy.

'You sort of feel,' said the Australian, 'that we ought to be over there, rather than sampling the flesh-pots here.'

'We could be pretty busy here, too, soon,' said Maxwell, 'if things go the way we're expecting.'

Mrs Cunningham was on the other side of the room.

There wasn't a ring of Australians 'round her.

She started coming across to them. Owen began to move away.

'For Christ's sake,' said Maxwell, 'don't all of you abandon me!'

The Prince, having failed to detach Zeinab, had moved elsewhere and was now talking to a group of senior British advisers from the various ministries. They knew, of course, who he was and treated him with the punctilious deference that was, in the British, so deceptive.

At the end of the evening, as he was leaving, he glanced back at his hosts.

'A strange people, don't you think,' he said to Owen. 'Rather lacking in polish.'

'Some rough edges, certainly,' said Owen.

'Raw,' said the Prince, with satisfaction. 'That's what they are. Compared with us.'

He went out into the night.

Owen picked up Zeinab. She was glowing, and leaned back against him in the arabeah as they drove home.

'Why is it,' she said meditatively, 'that the English and the Australians are so different? The English always *place* you when they meet you. In terms of what class you belong to, or what race, or what nationality. Whereas the Australians don't seem to care anything about any of that.'

'Don't they?' said Owen. 'They see you very much as a woman. Isn't that a kind of placing?'

'Maybe,' conceded Zeinab. 'But I don't mind that.'

'What was Faruq saying to you?'

Zeinab cackled with laughter.

'He said: "What is a pretty Turkish girl like you doing, getting married to an Englishman?"'

'Turkish?' said Owen.

⁓

'Well, yes,' said Zeinab. 'I *am* Turkish. Sort of.'

Many Egyptians were 'sort of.' There were sort of Greek Egyptians, Italian Egyptians, Albanian Egyptians, Montenegrin Egyptians, and Levantine Egyptians of all origins and persuasions. But Zeinab was more 'sort of' than most.

Her mother had been a Circassian slave. And therefore fair. Zeinab, however, was dark; not only dark but definitely Arab. Her father, Nuri Pasha, attributed this to his own ancestry. 'A touch of the Bedawin somewhere,' he said to Owen. Nuri put this down to his grandmother. 'Wanton, dear boy, wanton!' he said admiringly. 'But then, shut up in the harem, on my grandfather's estate in the country, while he was away in Cairo for long spells, what can one expect?'

He himself was of Turkish descent. As were most of the Pashas, as was the Sultan himself. The whole ruling class of Egypt had come to the country originally as officers in the Ottoman army and had carved out a position and property for themselves in the service of Khedives who over the years had become more and more detached from their Ottoman origins and allegiances.

It was allegiance that counted now, thought Owen. In the end the Khedives had become so detached from their Ottoman overlords that they had become virtually independent. Their allegiance these days was to themselves. Which way would they jump if Turkey invaded? He knew what Zeinab's father would say: towards whichever side looked like winning, dear boy.

'Do you *feel* Turkish?' he asked Zeinab.

'No. But I don't feel British, either.'

'Well, you wouldn't.'

'I feel Egyptian,' said Zeinab. She sighed. 'And the funny thing is that these days I feel more Egyptian than I've ever done before.'

'Is it the war?'

'No. A bit, perhaps,' she amended. 'But only a bit.'

'Me? Marrying me?'

'I don't feel that you've taken me over, if that's what you're thinking,' said Zeinab. 'In fact, the other way: I feel that I've taken *you* over.'

'Well, I'm glad about that.'

'No,' said Zeinab, musing, as the arabeah pottered gently through streets that were white in the moonlight. 'No. It's perhaps that I'm just beginning to understand what I've left behind me.'

'What have you left behind you?'

Zeinab thought.

'Closeness,' she pronounced eventually. 'The closeness of a hugger-mugger little world of cousins and second cousins and honorary aunts and friends you chat to at the hairdresser's who might be related to you or might not but it doesn't matter, they're all part of the same tight little society which knows everything you do and has done ever since you were a little girl in harem.'

'Well, look, you don't have to give that world up. You don't have to leave it behind you just because you've married me.'

Zeinab thought some more.

'It's not so much,' she said, 'that I've given it up as that it's given up me.'

'What do you mean?'

Zeinab shrugged.

'Well,' she said, 'it makes a difference, you know, if you marry an Englishman.'

They had always known that it would be harder for her than for him. He would always have his work, and although the Administration might not like it, they were unlikely, certainly at the moment, to want to dispense with someone capable. Life, for Owen, would go on pretty much as it had done before.

But for a woman it was more difficult. It was difficult anyway for a woman who wished to move outside the usual patterns of Egyptian society. 'Cupboards,' Zeinab described them as. 'As you grow up, you find that you're in a cupboard. And then when you marry, you find that you've been put in another cupboard. And stowed away in a back room.'

She had always fought, even when she was a child, against the fate she could see coming. Her father's indulgence, and the fact that he was a Pasha had given her a leeway unusual for Egyptian women and she had made the most of it. But she had felt the weight of the expectations always there, even when she was defying them, and had feared that in the end the walls of the cupboard would close in on her. It was partly, perhaps, in a last, desperate attempt to resist that that she had married Owen; knowing that once she had done that, she would never be able to go back. Knowing, too, or thinking that she knew, the kinds of exclusions, shuttings down, and cutting off that she would face.

'I'm sorry,' said Owen.

She shrugged.

'I knew what I was doing. I wanted to escape. I wanted to put that world behind me. I never thought I'd miss it. But, do you know,' she said, almost in surprise, 'lately I've been finding that I do.'

'It's not so surprising.'

'So when they shut me out,' she said, 'it hurts. I never thought I'd mind. But I do,' she said. 'I do.'

Chapter Six

The Camel Market was not really even on the edge of the city but further out. It was out beyond Mena House, near where a line of palm trees marked the limit of the Inundation. Owen was thinking about this as he strolled among the little pyramids of onions and hillocks of grain, and along the line of squatting figures with gaudy cottons spread out around them.

The people who came here were not city people but fellahin from the village up the road or else Arabs in from the desert. It was Bedawin women, with gold coins and coral chains dangling from their headbands, who were sauntering up and down and peering at the scarlet, coral-seeming celluloid beads, and Arish tribesmen, hawk-faced and sun-blackened, who were squatting round the tray of the market eating place and leaning across to dip their bread into the gravy.

A city man would be a fish out of water here: especially at night and among the animals. Owen just couldn't see it, see any of the toughs that he knew, the ones who usually did the killings, coming out here at night and making their way through the Market in the darkness and in among the camels to lie in wait for Sabri. Not even if they had been paid for it. They were uncomfortable out of their territories. The Camel Market would have seemed like the other side of the moon.

Even if it had been some individual with a grievance, Owen still couldn't see it. Why go to the trouble of coming out here? Why make things difficult for yourself?

But if not a city killer, then who? Someone familiar with the Market? One of the camel herdsmen, perhaps? He had to come back to them. They had denied it, but were they to be believed? There were Englishmen who accorded the Bedawin a blind romantic trust and took their word for binding. But Owen was not one of them. Nevertheless, on this occasion, he felt inclined to accept their word.

One of the other Bedawin, the Arish, maybe? He had spoken to some of them during the morning. They inhabited a different part of the desert from the one that Sabri had frequented and appeared to know nothing of him. That did not rule them out. One of them might have been hired for the job. But it seemed unlikely.

One of the villagers, then, who brought their produce to the market? He had been speaking to them, too. Sabri was unknown, both in the village and in the Market. He had always left for home the day he had arrived, the moment he had been paid. Again it seemed unlikely.

The villagers returned to their village every evening. But there were some Market people who stayed in the Market overnight, sleeping on the ground: the sellers of cottons and of the celluloid beads, for example. One of these was the fiki.

No, he told Owen, he had not heard anything during the night and certainly not at the back of his booth. He had been sleeping the sleep of the devout: would that others could say the same!

Owen took him to be referring to Sabri's killer but he was not. He was talking about the small boys of the Market.

Mention of the small boys suggested a new avenue of enquiry for Owen and he spoke to them later. Yes, they said eagerly, they had heard noises; and from the fiki's booth, too! It emerged, however, that they were only the usual noises that occurred when Marryam was there. As one avenue closed, another possible one opened: might Marryam have heard something? Well, no, said the small boys sadly. She had left with them and they had walked back to the village together.

There appeared to be something of a feud between the fiki and the small boys. The fiki said they were lacking in respect.

And he seemed more than half inclined to blame them for the body having been put where it had been. If not them, then the 'vile Bedawin.' And if not them, then Ali Saqi. Ali Saqi? Ali Saqi, it appeared, was a rival who sometimes encroached on the fiki's territory.

One thing was clear, said the fiki, whoever was to blame: there had been a lack of respect. It showed a lack of respect to put the body there in the first place. But what had followed was even worse.

'They took the body away,' he said.

'I'm sorry?'

'The man from the Parquet. He took the body away. He shouldn't have done that.'

'But, surely—?'

'He ought to have left it. For the family.'

'Well, I daresay, but in the heat—'

'No one minds a bit of a smell. And they would have come soon enough.'

'Well, yes, but—'

'If they'd left the body here, instead of taking it away, the family would have had to come here, wouldn't they? And then they would have seen me. Right on the spot. They would certainly have asked me.'

'Asked you—?'

'To speak the Holy Words of the funeral.'

'Oh, I see.'

He understood it now. The fiki relied for his income not just on the contributions of passers-by but also, and much more significantly, on what he could earn from reciting the scriptures at weddings and funerals.

'Now some other bastard will get the money,' said the fiki gloomily. 'I call it thoughtless. Really lacking in respect.'

Owen left him and walked back through the Market. The Bedawin, like the last of the camels they had brought, and the Levantine's donkeys, had departed the day before, leaving behind them only the charred embers of their fires and, where the camels had been, heaps of dung drying rapidly in the sun, snatches of camel wool caught to the tethering posts, and, over in one corner, clippings from where the donkey-barber had been plying his trade.

⚬⚬⚬

'Busy?' said Curtis. 'I'm rushed off my feet! It's this big build-up on the Canal. They want everything: tents, latrines, blocks for the gun emplacements—you try finding concrete blocks in the desert, old chap! All got to be fetched, and that means, at this short notice, buying them in from outside. These chaps—' he nodded towards the crowded tables—'are having a field day. Wood, paraffin, flour, you name it. It's all got to be supplied. People forget about that sort of thing, you know, but an army depends upon it. Well, you won't find me letting them down.'

'Glad to hear it,' said Owen, scanning the tables for Georgiades.

'It's a huge effort. You won't believe how big it is. Vast. But, of course, we in Supplies are well placed to know. We know what's going up and what's gone up. So we've got a pretty good idea of what will be there on the day.'

'Day?' said Owen vaguely. Where the hell was Georgiades?

'The day the Turks come over.'

'Oh, yes. Yes. Of course.'

'They'll get an almighty shock, I can tell you. When they find out what's facing them.'

The dummy camps flashed into Owen's mind.

'I think that's very likely, yes,' he said.

'Well, got to go. I expect you're just as busy as I am. How is it going?'

'How is it going?'

'Still working on him?' Curtis gave him a broad wink. 'No need to tell me, old chap. I know how it is. Once you've got one, you pretty soon get the rest of the ring.'

⚬⚬⚬

'What she needs is a good hiding,' said Garvin. Garvin was the Commandant of the Cairo Police and one of the old school.

'Maybe. But what she's going to get is a full-blown court appearance.'

'Do her good,' said Garvin unpromisingly. Owen had always known that this was going to be difficult. 'Scare the silliness out of her.'

'Or encourage it. What she wants, she says, is to be made a martyr of. Then everyone will see how the British treat Egyptians.'

'One of those, is she?' said Garvin. 'She sounds a right little pain in the ass. I don't know why you're spending time on her.'

'She's had enough time spent on her already,' said Owen. 'I don't want to see any more.'

'Well, I don't know that I can help you,' said Garvin. 'And I'm not sure that I want to. It sounds as if a court appearance might do her good.'

Owen sighed inwardly. Really, Garvin was getting very conservative these days. There had been a time when he had had a pretty good feeling for the way in which Egyptians would take things.

'It seems a bit excessive, that's all. A minor. First offence.'

'The court will take that into account, I daresay,' said Garvin. 'Why don't you leave it to them? It's a mistake being too soft. Especially with the young. It only makes trouble for later. And, by God, there's plenty of it around these days. I don't know what's come over the young.'

'That's more or less what her father said.'

'Oh, yes?' said Garvin indifferently.

'Yes. I like her father. Very capable, too. I saw him in action the other day at a fire.'

'Fire?' said Garvin.

'Yes. He's Head of the Fire Brigade.'

'Mohammed Sekhmet?'

'Yes.'

'Well, he's all right,' said Garvin, sitting up. 'Known him for years. It's his daughter? Why the hell didn't you say?'

❧

'Georgiades has been in,' said Nikos, looking up from his desk.

'Yes, I asked him to look in. He's made some actual contacts now and I wanted you to check them out.'

'One of them's Swedish. I don't have anything on him. He never stays in the country long, just in and out. I've passed his name on to London. They may have something on him.'

'He's the potential buyer, I take it?'

'Yes.'

'And the potential seller?'

'He's not really the seller, he's just a middle man. His name is Iskander and he sets up deals in commodities: grain, tobacco, sugar, that kind of thing.'

'Cotton?'

'Not up till now. But of course it's only now, with the new wartime regulations, that it's become worth it.'

'Do we have any idea where he'd be getting the cotton from?'

Nikos shook his head.

'It will be a Pasha. But we don't know which.'

The Pashas, the big landlords of the country, with their vast fields of cotton, were the ones whom the authorities found difficult to regulate. With the farmers of the Delta there was no problem. Their crops were small and easily accounted for. But on the huge estates of the pashas there was always scope for some part of the crop to go missing.

'Can we find out?'

Nikos thought.

'You could ask Georgiades to press Iskander. He won't get the identity of the Pasha but he might get the part of the country. Tell him to ask about the quality of the cotton, what its characteristics are. He could ask for a sample.'

'Right,' said Owen, 'I'll do that.'

As he went out, Nikos said, 'Georgiades wasn't looking too well.'

'It's all that damned drinking he's doing in the hotel!' said Owen uncharitably.

༺∞༻

Owen had a message from someone he knew in the Parquet, suggesting that they meet for a coffee. He guessed that the invitation was not accidental and wondered what it was that Mahmoud wanted to see him about.

They met in a café in the Ataba el Khadra, the big square which was the starting point for most of Cairo's trams, both the new electric ones and the old horse-drawn buses mostly used by black-gowned, heavily veiled women with huge baskets, and humming with people at any hour of the day or night. The tables of the cafés covered the pavements and sprawled out over the road and were always full. The road itself was jammed with pedestrians and vendors selling things to them: peanuts and sugar cane, pastries and seditious newspapers. If you couldn't find a particular Nationalist newspaper that you wanted—unlikely in Cairo—you could always find it here. The cries of the vendors mingled with the shouts of frustrated arabeah drivers, the bleating of sheep, the clanging of the bells of the trams, and, from time to time, the despairing notes of the handbell at the front of a fire engine desperately trying to force its way out of the fire station at the corner of the square and through the packed throng.

Mahmoud jumped up from a table and greeted him warmly, throwing his arms round him in the ebullient Arab fashion.

'You are well, yes? And Zeinab?'

'Well, too, God be praised. And you yourself? and Aisha?'

They sat down and chatted. This was a favourite rendezvous for them both: Mahmoud, because it was on neutral ground and did not imply Parquet recognition of the office of Mamur Zapt (the Parquet refused on principle to accept that there should be such a thing as the Sultan's Secret Police, much less a British-headed Secret Police), Owen because he liked the buzz of the cafés.

Eventually Mahmoud got round to it.

'You are interested in one of our cases, yes?'

'The murder in the Camel Market, yes.'

'We have put Hassan Marbri on to it. He is a promising young man but this is his first case.'

'He seems to have made a good start.'

'You think so?' Mahmoud was pleased. He identified totally with his work at the Parquet and couldn't bear any falling short.

'Yes. Although I think that he may not have realised that the Bedawin were likely to move away.'

Mahmoud did not take this up. Instead, he said, 'We gave him this case because we thought it was uncomplicated.'

Owen could guess now what lay behind the meeting. It was the point Marbri had picked up. Why was Owen interested? The Mamur Zapt normally confined himself to cases with a political aspect. But anything that was political in Cairo was highly unlikely to be uncomplicated. The Parquet, anxiously watching over its own, had been concerned.

Owen's acquaintance with Mahmoud was long-standing and their relationship good; not only good, close. He would have to tell him the truth.

'The man who was killed was one of mine,' he said.

'Ah!'

'One of mine in a very minor way but still mine.'

'I see.' Mahmoud began to back off. He didn't want to know anything about the clandestine side of Owen's activities. Too often they had a Nationalist target; and Mahmoud himself was a strongly committed member of the Nationalist Party. 'Do you want us to leave it all to you?'

'No. It may be nothing at all to do with the work he did for me. Which was, as I say, very minor. It would be better to treat it as an entirely normal case, to be investigated entirely in the normal way.'

Mahmoud relaxed.

'If you think so,' he said.

'We could, perhaps, share what we find out.'

'Well, certainly.'

'All I want to know is who killed him. And why. And then, well, if it's nothing to do with me, I'm happy to leave it entirely to Marbri.'

'Well, that is as it should be,' said Mahmoud, satisfied.

He said something else but Owen was unable to catch it because of the particularly violent clanging of a bell in the street right beside them. A fire engine had come to an absolute stop.

'Make way! Make way!'

A gap opened. The driver was about to move into it when an arabeah darted into it ahead of him.

'This is foolishness!' cried the driver of the fire engine angrily.

The people at the nearest tables gave him sympathetic support.

'How would you like it if it was your house?' they shouted to the arabeah driver.

Some firemen sleeping on the pavement in front of the fire station jumped up and ran down into the road.

'Get out of the way, you stupid bastard!'

Two of them caught the horses' heads and pulled the arabeah to one side.

'Hey, what do you think you're doing?' cried the arabeah driver.

One of the firemen went up to him and told him. The driver began to climb down out of the arabeah. The arabeah's passenger joined his shouts to the exchanges.

The fire engine moved on past, the driver leaning across to add his voice to those of his colleagues. It succeeded in forcing a way through the crowd and turned up one of the side streets.

The firemen let go of the arabeah's horses and moved back to speak to its driver. He changed his mind and climbed back up into his seat and gave his horses a sharp cut of his whip. Startled, they plunged ahead and nearly into a huge porter singlehandedly carrying a piano across his shoulders. As he turned round, the end of the piano hit the arabeah. The passenger inside gave an anguished cry. The watchers at the end of the tables cheered.

Eventually the arabeah managed to get away. The tables settled down, and the firemen returned to their positions on the pavement. It was the kind of event seen many times a day in the Ataba; one of the reasons, indeed, why the tables were always crowded.

'There do seem a lot of fires these days,' said Mahmoud.

'It's the heat, said Owen. 'Everything's as dry as tinder.'

The incident, though, had recalled something to his mind. He told Mahmoud about Yasmin.

'I've got Garvin to agree,' he said. 'He's prepared to drop proceedings if the Parquet is.'

'I don't think there will be any doubt about that,' said Mahmoud drily. 'Not if she's being proceeded against for distributing material sympathetic to the Nationalist Party.'

He said he would see to the formalities himself when he got back to his office. Then, seeing that Owen still looked doubtful, he said: 'What's the matter? There'll be no problem. I'm sure they'll agree to it.'

'They may agree to it,' said Owen. 'But will she?'

He told Mahmoud about his interview with Yasmin.

'A foolish girl!' said Mahmoud. 'Her father should speak to her.'

'Ye-es,' said Owen. 'I think he's tried.'

He was in the middle of telling Mahmoud about Mohammed Sekhmet when the idea came to him. He broke off.

'Do you think I could speak to Aisha?' he said.

Mahmoud, old friend of Owen's though he was, was taken aback. One thing you did *not* do in Egypt was ask to speak to another man's wife.

'In your presence, of course,' said Owen hastily. 'You see, I think she could be just the person to help. The girl is still at school. At the Sanieh, in fact. Wasn't that where Aisha was?'

She had been. And not very long before, either. Mahmoud had married Aisha straight from school, only a few months ago.

'The girl might listen to her,' said Owen, 'even if she won't listen to anyone else.'

⌀⟋

As he was going home that evening he heard a loud burst of drunken singing. It came from the Wagh el Birket. He hesitated for a moment and then turned up the Sharia Bab el Bahri towards it. A group of drunken soldiers was standing in front of one of the houses. They had their arms around each other's shoulders and were singing loudly. Owen could make out the words. Fortunately no one else could.

The soldiers hitched themselves drunkenly together and staggered down the street towards him. Some of them were clutching beer bottles. One of them threw an empty bottle away and it broke into pieces against a wall.

Owen had no intention of interfering. Whether he had authority to do so was questionable. The Mamur Zapt's writ did not extend to the military. But whether he had authority or not, Owen wasn't daft enough to get involved. He was dressed in mufti and they were unlikely to be inclined to listen to any civilian; or anyone in uniform, for that matter.

They weaved out of sight. The Military Police would soon pick them up. Unless they were too busy with all the others.

The soldiers were Australian and had 'wounded' stripes on. Not too wounded, presumably, although he was not going to be too disparaging. They had probably come from Gallipoli. Well, good luck to them.

All the same, something was bothering him. He knew what it was. It was that such behaviour was very unusual in Cairo streets. Muslims didn't get drunk. Well, that wasn't completely true. Working men, in the city as in the village, liked a pot of marissa beer. Selim, the big constable at the Bab-el-Khalk, liked several. But they very rarely got drunk, and then only at parties or family celebrations, weddings, for instance. Most Muslims didn't drink at all.

It came home to him how such behaviour must appear to Egyptians: to the austere Mahmoud, for instance, or the strict Mohammed Sekhmet. And there were many like them. They were, in fact, in the majority. The Wagh el Birket was hardly typical of Cairo but even here people averted their eyes and walked past uncomfortably.

Perhaps he had dismissed a little too easily the representations of the Mufti and the Sultan. In this at least they were probably speaking to their people.

He went along the street to the house outside which the soldiers had been standing and from which they had probably emerged. And, yes, it was a liquor house.

He went in. A man came up to him.

'What would you like, Effendi!'

'I'd like to speak to the manager.'

'He is, alas, not here.'

'Right. I'll wait.'

He soon appeared.

'Are you the owner?'

'Not I, Effendi.'

The owner was someone else. He was Maltese. And tomorrow he would be Greek, and the day after, Italian. It was the old Egyptian story.

But old stories can have a new twist, and Owen knew what this one was. It was the influx into Egypt of thousands of newcomers bringing with them different customs, different assumptions, differing values. Bringing with them, too, the money that could create suppliers to meet their needs. Places like this liquor house, for example. The Egyptians liked the money, but they didn't like what it was doing to them.

Chapter Seven

'Salt,' said Owen's orderly, preoccupied. 'I've got to go out, Effendi. We're still two rotls short.'

'Salt?' said Owen. 'What do you want salt for?'

'Ahmed is making up a load, Effendi, which his cousin is going to take up to the Canal and sell. They say you can make ten piastres a rotl there. We've already got twenty rotls, so that will be...What will it be, Effendi?'

'Two hundred piastres. And twenty, if you get another two rotls. But, look, are you sure they want salt?'

'Oh, yes, Effendi, everyone wants salt.'

'You don't think they'll have some already?'

'Oh, no, Effendi. There are so many men there. They're bound to run short. And if they don't want it, Ahmed's cousin can always sell it to the Turks.'

༺∞༻

It seemed to Owen that everybody was doing it. Go into the bazaars and the talk was all of the great rewards to be had from selling to the Army at the Canal. In the souk the stall holders calculated the benefit of the higher prices at the Canal and contemplated moving. In the orderly rooms of the Ministries others besides Owen's orderly were discussing speculative ventures. And at the tables of the cafés in the Ataba el Khada young effendi from the Credit Lyonnais, the Banque Ottoman, and the other great commercial enterprises nearby gathered every evening to assess the ways in which a private piastre might be turned to their advantage.

Nor was activity confined to the theoretical. Every morning lines of people taking things to the Canal straggled out of the city in the direction of the Ismailiya road, some on camels, some on donkeys, most on foot. The loads they bore were often bizarre, testifying more to the Egyptian experience of tourists and their eternal optimism than to perceptions of economic or military reality. There were columns of tarbooshes nodding gently from the backs of donkeys, brightly coloured balloons floating eerily above the backs of camels, men festooned with brushes and covered with leather belts and braces and whips; knick-knacks from the bazaars, oleographs straight from the railings in front of the hotels; ostrich feathers and birds in cages. It was as if all the street sellers of Cairo had suddenly decided to transfer themselves and their wares elsewhere. The effect was as of a carnival procession.

Some of the traffic was less speculative. The Camel Market was now serving as a collection point for the camels and donkeys coming in from all over Egypt. So great were the numbers that the Bedawin had not been allowed to return to the west but were being used to bring the animals in. They despised the work but the money was good.

From the Camel Market the animals were despatched to the front, travelling in great herds along the Ismailiya road. It was there that one morning Owen found someone he knew.

'Hello, Effendi!' said the donkey-barber.

'Why, hello! You have taken your friends, then, at their word.'

'If the mountain will not come to Anji, then Anji must go to the mountain,' said the donkey-barber, grinning.

'I would have thought there was still plenty of work for you in the Market,' said Owen.

'There is, but there won't be for long. Soon all the donkeys in Egypt will be at the Canal.'

'Well, I hope you make your fortune.'

'That will be the day!' said the donkey-barber.
They walked along a little together.
'Are you still searching for Sabri's killer, Effendi?'
'I am.'
'And have you found him?'
'Not yet.'
'Perhaps you are not searching in the right place.'
'Is not the Camel Market the right place?'
'It is where he died, certainly.'
'Then—?'
'Sabri was a little man, Effendi. And it was probably a little man that killed him. But these days, although it is the little men who die, it is the big men that appoint their deaths. In the Camel Market as on the Canal.'

In the old days before the war, work in the big Government offices would stop for the day at two. It would start early, often at seven, but finish before the heat became too intolerable. These days, however, with the pressure of the war, people often worked through till five or six. This was what Owen normally did, but this afternoon a couple of meetings had been cancelled and he was finding it hard to work in his office because of the heat and he went home.

He found Zeinab lying listlessly on the bed.
'What's the matter?' he said.
'Nothing's the matter,' she said, standing up.

They took their lunch up on to the roof where it was cooler. A previous owner had created a little garden there. Trellis work covered with runner beans and pots with shrubs provided some shade and there was just enough breeze coming across the roofs to make it pleasant.

'What have you been doing?'
Zeinab shrugged.
'Nothing.'
'Not been out?'
'What's the point?'

This was not like Zeinab. In the old days she would have been out doing the rounds of the galleries and dropping in on people she knew.

Or so Owen imagined. He suddenly realised that he didn't know how Zeinab had spent her mornings before they had got married. He had gone off to work and had taken for granted that she would be doing something of her own.

'Nothing on in the galleries?'

'Not since the war.'

'What are they all doing?'

Zeinab had a lot of artist friends. They had to be mildly Bohemian, and either disreputable or relaxed about proprieties, depending on how you looked at it, to allow an independent woman to mix with them.

'Ah!' said Zeinab.

'What do you mean?'

Zeinab shrugged again.

'Well, they're not getting commissions. They're finding it hard to get work to do. And so, well, some of them have gone back to their villages, some have gone abroad, to Damascus or Smyrna, in the hope of finding jobs—'

'Isn't that difficult? With the Turks there?'

'The Turks don't bother them. Anyway, it's all one big area, the Levant. Not exactly a continuation of Egypt, or of Turkey, for that matter, but a sort of common area where frontiers don't matter.'

'And so that's where they've gone?'

'That's right. The war's an irrelevance from their point of view. A nuisance wished on them by others.'

'Hum. And so they've all gone, and there's no one for you to talk to. What about Samira?'

'You're forgetting. Samira doesn't talk to me these days.'

'Yes, but—'

Zeinab shrugged once more.

'I can get by,' she said.

'Staying at home? Isn't that—' he tried to remember the expression she had used—'just another cupboard?'

'Yes.'

'Well, look, I don't want you to be shut up. If your own circles have pushed you away, that doesn't have to be an end to it. Why don't I introduce you to—'

'A few Mrs Cunninghams? Thanks.'

'They're not all like her.'

'I know what they're like. And I think they're as much in cupboards as I am. I don't want to spend my time playing bridge. Or going down to the Club. Or taking tea.'

'Well, no.'

'I'll tell you what it is. They're appendages. That's all they are. They're appendages to their husbands. And that's not very different from what Egyptian women are. All right, you're allowed to see English women, they're not shut away in some back room. But they don't have a life apart from their husbands. Sorry, I didn't quite mean it like that, I meant there ought to be them *and* their husbands, not just their husbands with them somehow hanging on.'

'Yes, well, I see that.'

'Do you know what I think it is? I think that it's work. You're all right, you've got a job. If somebody wants something, something to do with work, that is, they've got to go to you. They've got to admit you're there. But if you're a woman, they don't *have* to recognise your existence, they can look right past you.'

'Listen, why don't I have a word with Cairns-Grant? I'm sure he could find a—'

'I want work,' said Zeinab. 'But I don't want it to be a British gift. That's not right. It's got to be Egyptian.'

'Yes, but—'

'Yes, I know. There aren't any jobs for Egyptian women. So I'm going to do something else. I'm going to go to the university.'

These were women students at the new university. A few. They had to attend separate classes from the men—you couldn't have men and women together, that would be improper—and the range of subjects they could do was limited.

'What would you study?'

'That's a problem,' Zeinab admitted. 'There's only ethics and psychology. And some lectures on hygiene and infant care. But I don't want to know about infant care. That's preparing me for motherhood, and that's a kind of cupboard too. That leaves ethics and psychology. I think I'll go for ethics.'

'You won't be able to start immediately. You'll have to wait for the new academic year.'

'Oh, I'll fix that,' said Zeinab, with a flash of her old confidence.

'I thought you were supposed to be studying ethics?'

'All proceeding to plan,' said Cavendish.

It was the Intelligence Committee again and they were back where they had left off at their previous meeting: on the construction of dummy bases.

'Well, is it?' said Lawrence. 'I went there and I couldn't see anything.'

'Well, you wouldn't, would you?' said one of the Army officers. 'Not if they're imaginary.'

'They can't be completely imaginary. Or else the Turks will see there's nothing there.'

'I thought we were supposed to be building false roads and things?' said Paul.

'Well, we are. But it takes time.'

'If it takes too much time, it'll be too late,' said Lawrence.

'The trouble is, we haven't got the labour.'

'Of course we've got the labour! We've got half the bloody Army there, haven't we?'

'Ah, yes, but they're all busy building the *real* bases.'

There was a little silence.

'What about using civilians?' said one of the officers.

'There's the whole Egyptian population in theory,' said another.

'Yes, but—' began Owen.

'They haven't exactly rushed forward,' said Cavendish.

'Is it a question of wages?' asked one of the officers.

'Not exactly,' said Owen. 'The fact is, there's a deep-rooted reluctance among the fellahin to volunteer for anything. It goes back to the time when they were volunteered by the Pashas into working for part of each year on the dams and canals.'

'Well, that's a poor show,' said the senior Army representative. 'Have they no sense of public spirit?'

'I think they would prefer to be working on their own land.'

'Yes, but there's a war on!'

'I don't think they see it as their war,' said Paul.

'Well, we've got to do something. We can't divert soldiers. This is essentially a construction job and we ought to use civilians.'

'They should be good at digging, shouldn't they?' said another of the officers. 'I mean, if they've worked on the land!'

'And on the canals,' supported another officer.

'They could dig trenches as well,' offered a third.

'Damned useful!' said the senior officer.

'Maybe,' said Cavendish, 'but, just at the moment, they don't seem very interested.'

'If they won't volunteer of their own accord...' began another officer.

'...perhaps someone could do it for them...?' finished a third.

'Are we talking about forced labour?' asked Paul.

'Well, I wouldn't put it quite like that—'

'But, yes, we are!' said Owen. 'And I don't like it. I don't think it will work. There's a long tradition of resistance to forced labour in Egypt, going back to the days of the corvée system which existed before the British arrival in the country, and which they abolished as soon as they did. Are you saying we should go back to that?'

'Well—'

'This is war time—'

'They would be damned useful—'

'Digging trenches.'

'We could expand the auxiliary Labour corps.'

There was already an Egyptian Labour Corps serving in the Dardenelles.

'They're doing damned well!' said the senior officer.

'Yes, but they're all volunteers,' said Owen. 'Genuine volunteers.'

'These would be,' said one of the officers. 'Once they got used to it.'

'It's going to cause trouble,' warned Owen.

He could see, however, that the feeling of the meeting was against him.

༄

The big constable caught him as he was about to go up the steps at the Bab-el-Khalk.

'Effendi,' he said, 'I seek your counsel.'

Owen stopped.

'Glad to help, Selim, if I can.'

'I am thinking of selling my wife, Effendi.'

'Well, I don't know, Selim, that is quite a step—'

'Not really, Effendi, I've got two more.'

'Yes, well—'

'You see, Effendi, I need the money.'

'Perhaps if you talk to Bimbashi McPhee he will give you an advance on your pay—'

'No, no, Effendi, I need more than that. And, besides, he's already given me an advance this month.'

'What exactly do you need the money for, Selim?'

'To make my fortune.'

'Yes, well—'

'No, no, Effendi, this is a good one. Everyone's doing it.'

'Look, Selim, if I were you—'

'No, no, Effendi, not this time. This is certain gain. What you do is buy something that's in short supply at the Canal. Then you take it over there and sell it at—oh, Effendi, the prices they say you can get at these new camps! You can't lose, Effendi, believe me!'

'Yes, I've heard that before.'

'No, really, it's just a case of hitting on the right things. Now, Effendi, this is what I wanted to ask you. You know these

Australians: what would be the right thing for them? I thought beer. Or perhaps hashish.'

'Go for beer. The Australians have not yet learned the delights of hashish. But—'

'Of course, I could always offer them my wife,' said Selim meditatively.

☙

Mahmoud had invited Owen round to his house that evening 'for drinks.' As an afterthought he also invited Zeinab. It wasn't his first thought because normally in Egypt when you invited a man out, he left his wife behind him. Mahmoud, however, viewed such a practice—and many other practices in Egypt—as not progressive, and Mahmoud was above all progressive. When he looked about him he could see many things in Egypt that he believed to be wrong and he put this down to the country's being locked into the past: locked by the Khedive and the pashas, but also by the British. He was, therefore, as a good Nationalist, committed to getting rid of both. However, he also wanted, passionately, Egypt to move forward and take an equal place with other, more developed, nations. He recognised that these did some things better than Egypt did; and perhaps—just perhaps—the way they regarded women was one of them. On consideration, then, he decided to invite Zeinab too.

The more he thought about this, the more he liked it. It would neatly solve the problem—he still, despite himself, felt it to be a problem—of allowing Owen to talk to his wife. By shifting the whole thing to the plane of the modern, where it was permissible for men to talk to other men's wives, he could smooth over all awkwardness. Not only that, it would help Aisha. Mahmoud was anxious that his wife be modern, too. Although not too modern.

The house was an old, dilapidated one just off the Sharia -el-Nahhasin and for years, ever since his father's death, Mahmoud had lived in it alone with his mother. Now, as was the custom—in Egypt, after marriage, the wife moved to the mother-in-law—Aisha had moved in and already the house felt different.

It was only a few weeks since Owen had been there and already he could see changes. The main reception room, on the first floor, had been spruced up. There was a new, brighter carpet on the wall. A particularly worn divan—the whole house had always seemed rather worn, running down as Mahmoud's mother had grown older—had been replaced by a new one. There were new leather cushions on the floor. There were bowls of sweet pea flowers everywhere. The house seemed to have come to life.

Aisha had changed, too, even in the few weeks since he had last seen her. She had grown plumper, rounder. Well, perhaps that was not surprising: girls did change a lot at that age. Or could that plumpness possibly be—? Surely not. He could sense Zeinab taking it in and felt uneasy.

Aisha had changed in other respects as well, coming forward confidently to greet them, unveiled, her hands outstretched. She knew Owen quite well, of course, or, at least, more than she knew any other man apart from her father and her husband. Even so, when he remembered how shy she had been only a short time ago, at the time of their marriage—

She sat down on one of the divans, Zeinab beside her, and Owen sat a proper distance away, on another. Mahmoud, a modern man this evening, fetched drinks. Lemon juice. A strict Muslim, he meant something different by drinks than what Owen did.

'Yasmin?' said Aisha. 'Yes, I remember her. She was in the year below me. She was always in trouble.'

'Well, she's in trouble again.'

He told her what had happened.

'The thing is, she's got caught up in the system. Quite unnecessarily. They ought not to have made so much of it. But with all this business about spies—'

'Spies?' said Mahmoud. 'A school girl?'

'Yes, I know. But, you see, now that she's in the system, unless we can do something, she'll never get out. It seems ridiculous, but that's the way—'

'Well, of course, if I can help,' said Aisha, 'I'd be glad to. But what is it you want me to do?'

'Have a word with her. You see, she won't listen to me. Or her father. Or the headmistress. Anyone in authority. But I thought that perhaps she might listen to you.'

'I doubt it,' said Aisha. 'Unless she has changed greatly. Well, I'm willing to talk to her. Or, at least, I might be. But what is it you want me to talk to her *about?*'

'Well, some sensible advice—'

'I'm not sure that she wants to listen to sensible advice. And what seems sensible to you may not seem so to her.'

'Well, that's the problem—'

'Or me, either,' said Aisha, 'if by that you mean trying to persuade her to give up political action which to me, frankly, seems quite legitimate.'

'I don't know that I do mean that. Just political action that is likely to get her into trouble.'

'What was she doing, exactly? Distributing political leaflets? Well, we've all done that.'

'Aisha!' said Mahmoud, shocked.

'Well, we have. When I was in the seniors we were passing them round all the time. I used to daub slogans on the walls.'

'Look, it's *because* you daubed slogans on the walls that I thought she might listen to you,' said Owen.

'Yes, but what is it exactly that you want me to tell her?'

'Not to make a martyr of herself. She is determined that it should go to court. Then everyone will see, she says, the oppressiveness of the system.'

'Well—'

'That is foolishness,' said Mahmoud. 'She is too young. A child. She does not realise the damage she will do to herself. It will affect her chances for life. For marriage, a career, if that's what she wants, and it sounds as if she might. She is too young. Let her leave politics until she is older.'

'Well—' said Aisha.

'I was thinking of her family as well as her,' said Owen. 'Her father came to see me.'

'I don't think I'd tell her that,' said Aisha.

'But why not?' said Mahmoud, turning to her. 'Surely she must recognise the duty she owes to her father?'

'Well—' said Aisha. 'What do you think?' she said to Zeinab.

Zeinab took time to consider. She wasn't quite sure what she thought. Her own upbringing had been so different from that of Yasmin, or Aisha, for that matter. In the larger household of a Pasha, fathers were remote figures and the question of the duty you owed them was invested with less intensity. And, besides, Nuri had not been exactly an ordinary pasha. He was an enthusiastic Francophile and when Zeinab's mother had died, he had brought his daughter up as much in French style as in Egyptian. He, too, in his way, was a moderniser.

All the same, Zeinab thought she could understand what it might mean to live in a family like this Yasmin. It would feel very like living in that close, claustrophobic world of the Egyptian elite that she herself lived in. And she could sense, and share, Aisha's reservations.

'I think she wants to be free,' she said.

Aisha nodded her head in satisfaction.

'I am sorry, I do not understand,' said Mahmoud. He wasn't quite sure what this was all about, but suddenly it seemed to matter. 'In what sense, "free"?' Ideas fired him up. As they did many Egyptians. That, for Owen, was one of the delights of Cairo café conversation. 'How can you cut yourself off from your father, your family, and be free? They are part of you, and you part of them. You cannot shed your duties to them in the way a lizard shakes off its skin.'

'I don't think she quite wants to do that,' said Owen. 'Anyway, I think that toying with shedding them is part of growing up.'

'Toying is all very well,' said Mahmoud, 'if it leads to a proper appreciation of the family and how much wisdom it contains. She should not go against her father.'

'Do you think that this "toying" applies to political ideas, too?' asked Aisha. 'Do you think that is what Yasmin is doing—toying with ideas which she will discard later? Because if you do, I think you are wrong. And it is not respectful, not respectful to her.'

'No,' said Zeinab.

'These ideas are serious to her. And not just to her. They are serious ideas. And you should not discount them. I will speak to Yasmin, yes, for I do not want her to be hurt. But if she insists that she wants her ideas taken seriously and believes that this is the only way they will be, then I shall not go against her.'

She *had* changed, thought Owen.

⚬⚬⚬

Georgiades was looking positively green.

'What the hell is the matter?'

'I'm shit scared.'

Owen had never seen him like this before.

'It's all right. I'll get someone round. He'll be right alongside you. Two of them, if that's what you want.'

'No, no, it's not that.'

'You don't need to worry. You're not on your own. I'll send Aziz round. Selim, too. He may not be bright but he's big. He's just the man for something like this.'

'No, no.'

'What's got into you? You're not usually like this. Look, I'll stay with you myself until the others get here.'

Georgiades shook his head despairingly.

'No,' he said, 'it's not that.'

'What the hell is it, then?'

'It's Rosa.'

'Rosa!'

'I told you she takes an interest in that sort of thing. Business.'

'Well?'

'She's going into it on her own. I've been telling her about all these blokes here and the way they're all on the make, the way they're shoving things up to the Canal as fast as they can go.'

'Well?'

'Well, she reckons if they can do it, so can she. And she's signed a contract—Jesus, the thought of it scares me, just the *thought* of it—to deliver a thousand ardabs of camel fodder to the Camel Corps detachments at the Canal. She fixed it up with someone in Supplies. A thousand ardabs!

"'You must be crazy," I said: "where the hell are you going to get a thousand ardabs of berseem from?" "Oh, that's all right," she said, "I've got that arranged." There's this village a few miles out of town and she's talked to the pasha's agent there and he's agreed to supply her. She's signed a contract for that, too!'

Georgiades beat his head.

'Contracts!' he said. 'Actually signed them! "Look," I said, "the one thing I know about lawyers—and, believe me, I've had some experience of them in my job—is that you don't let them trick you into signing any kind of contract. You don't sign *anything* when you've got a lawyer around. A contract is just a handle to screw you with. Believe me, I know!"'

"'No, you don't," she says. "I sign contracts for the family business every week when my father's away." Well, that's something I didn't know, and wouldn't have agreed to it if I had. Not that that would have done much good, she never listens to me. But that's what she's done, signed contracts for a thousand ardabs of camel fodder!

"'Where are you going to get the money?" I say. "Where are you going to get the money? This bloke's not going to give you berseem for nothing. Not if he's like any other Pasha's agent I know."

"'It's all right," she says. "I've got that figured out. It's in the contract. Payment for a quarter within a month, the rest to follow in six weeks." "A month?" I said. "Six weeks?" "Yes," she says. "By then I'll have the first payment in from the Camel Corps—that's in the contract, too, the one the Camel Corps has signed. And the rest will be in before the six weeks is up."'

"'It must be a hundred thousand piastres!"' I say. "A hundred and thirty," she says. "Don't forget my profit margin." "Yes, well, suppose it goes wrong? I only get four hundred piastres a week!" "It won't go wrong," she says. "Go back to sleep!"

'I wish I could go back to sleep, I can tell you. I lie awake at nights thinking about it. A thousand ardabs! A hundred thousand piastres! She must be crazy.

'I can't bear to think about it. It gets me down. I've never been much good with money. I don't like to think about it. It comes in and it goes out. That's all I know about it and all I want to know. Anything more terrifies me. I give her my money at the end of each week and say: "Okay, you handle it. Give me something from time to time, and the rest is up to you." And now she does this!

'What will we do if it doesn't work out? I've got a house, I've got a kid. What will we do? Oh, my God,' said Georgiades, 'I feel terrible.'

Chapter Eight

Even from his office Owen could hear it. There seemed to be some disturbance in the yard below. Women's voices, men's voices, raised in altercation. A few moments later Owen's orderly came in, his face flushed.

'Effendi, there is a nuisance in the yard. Some crazy woman. She wants to see you. Abdul asks, what is her business? She says her business is with you, not with him. He says, everyone wants to see the Mamur Zapt—this is not quite true, Effendi—and he, Abdul, needs to be sure that they are not time wasters; so what is her business? She says, she hasn't time to waste on him, she needs to see the Mamur Zapt now, at once. He asks her her business again and she tries to push past him. He says, okay, you daft bitch, then you can wait. So she kicks him in the balls. Ibrahim and Mustapha seek to restrain her but this is difficult because she is fighting and biting and scratching. We have to call for Selim. She tries to bite him too but he knows how to hold her. I will say this for him, he really knows how to handle a woman. However, Effendi, she has just kneed him in the balls, too, and I really think it would be best if you came—' It was Sabri's widow.

'It's all right, you can let her go.'

'Effendi, are you sure? She is some wild woman—'

'That's all right. Let her go.'

She shook herself free and stood panting and sobbing.

'Come with me.'

He started to lead her up to his office but she seized him by the arm and said: 'There is not time!'

'What is the matter?'

'My son!' she said. 'He has gone to the Camel Market to seek out the Bedawin. He says, if Ahmed will not demand satisfaction from them, then he will! But, Effendi, they will kill him. He is just a boy.'

'Be easy. The Bedawin are not there.'

'They are, Effendi. They have returned. One spoke of it in the village. He had seen them with their camels. And foolish people in the village began to murmur, and say: "They walk comfortably, while Sabri lies dead." But Salah, my son, said: "I will not let this be so." And he ran for his knife, and I tried to reason with him, but he shook me off. He seized Shukri's donkey and rode off for the city, and now, Effendi, I fear for him.'

'I will go at once. Selim, get an arabeah. And you'd better come with me.'

'You must save him, Effendi. You owe me this. Did not his father die on your business? Must the son die, too?'

❦

The Bedawin were indeed back. He could see them on the other side of the Market, busy with a new lot of camels. They seemed to be having some trouble. The camels were pitching and tossing and threatening to break away. The Bedawin were cursing and running round with their whips. He could see no sign, fortunately, of the boy.

When he got closer he saw what the trouble was about. A huge bull camel was in rut—you could tell by the pink, balloon-like bladder, the size of a football, inflated from the side of its mouth. It was milling about and making a nuisance of itself. The Bedawin were trying to separate it from the other camels. It was biting and snapping at them. Someone managed to get a rope over its head and then a silsil chain. Owen hoped it wouldn't break. A great bull camel like this was immensely strong. Eventually the Bedawin managed to get some hobbles on.

'We should have left this one behind,' said one of the Bedawin, wiping his sleeve across his face to mop up the sweat.

'It's a good camel, though, and will fetch a good price.'

'We could have picked it up next time.'

'There won't be a next time. We've just about cleared the place out.'

'We've just about cleared the country out, I should think. There can't be many good camels left.'

'A good job, too. Now we can go home.'

'There'll be plenty of camels there,' said Owen.

'If the Senussi haven't got them.'

He had a moment to spare.

'You're having problems with the Senussi again?'

There were always problems in the west with the Senussi. They were a large confederation of tribes based for the most part in Libya, but borders were elastic in that area and they were always raiding across into Egypt and the Sudan.

'Not exactly problems this time. It's just that when we left, there were quite a few of them about.'

'They said they wanted to buy camels. It had been a bad year for breeding so far as they were concerned and they needed to replenish their stock. They were willing to pay good prices, they said.'

'If they really are prepared to pay good prices, then I don't mind. But Sabri said that was a lot of nonsense. He'd heard some of them talking and it was just an excuse. They hadn't brought any money with them.'

'Well, if they weren't thinking of paying for them, then the sooner we get back, the better.'

'You know, I thought I might ride ahead and—'

He stopped. He was looking at something on the other side of the Market. All the other Bedawin were turning round.

It was the boy. He was standing there, brandishing a dagger and shouting at the Bedawin nearest him.

Owen started across. The other Bedawin followed him.

'What the hell is this?' someone said.

'I defy you!' the boy was shouting. 'Choose your man and send him out!'

'Run along, lad!' someone said.

'You are men without honour! I have always heard that the Bedawin were men. Now I know that is not true!'

'Now look, lad—'

'Shut your mouth!' It was the one who had spoken truculently to Owen when he had first asked them about Sabri. He began to walk towards the boy, feeling for his knife.

'Leave him!' Owen shouted. 'He's Sabri's boy!'

'Sabri's boy!'

The man stopped for a moment.

'He shouldn't speak like that,' he said.

'He means nothing by it. He doesn't know what he is doing. He is but a boy!'

'Yes, but—All the same, he shouldn't speak like that.'

'Why does he have to speak like that to us?'

'Fools have been speaking to him. They say you have refused compensation.'

'Compensation? What the hell have we got to pay compensation *for?*'

'He thinks we did it.'

'Did the hell *what?*'

'Killed Sabri.'

'But we've *told* them we didn't. Don't they believe us?'

'That's bloody insulting!'

'He ought not to speak to us like that,' said the truculent one, moving forward again.

'He is just a boy!' cried Owen. 'Misled by foolish men!' He ran between them. 'He is Sabri's son. Sabri, who rode with you!' He suddenly became angry. 'Kill him,' he said, 'and then, indeed, men will say you are without honour!'

'Here—'

'Effendi,' muttered Selim, 'bethink you—'

Several of the men were now heading towards them, their hands on their belts.

There were policemen in the Market, but they were hanging back. And there were soldiers, too, the Levantine's ones, in with the camels. But they were prudently keeping their distance.

'He is Sabri's son, Sabri, who was one of you!'

'He was *not* one of us.'

'He rode with you.'

'That's not the same thing.'

'He shouldn't speak like that,' said the man. 'Not to us.'

He suddenly stepped forward. Owen stood in his way. The man thrust at Owen with his knife. Selim, possibly foolishly, as he told the orderly room later that afternoon, but bravely, as he also told the orderly room, struck him on the arm with his truncheon. The Bedawin cried out in pain—Selim was a big man and apprehension made him hit hard—and dropped his knife on the ground.

The other Bedawin moved in.

Owen snatched the boy's knife from him and threw that on the ground too.

'An unarmed boy!' he cried, 'the son of a man who rode with you! I did not believe this of the Bedawin. I took you for men of honour!'

'So we are!'

'But—'

Owen looked round desperately. He saw the men who had talked to him at the fire and suddenly their names flashed into his mind.

'Wajja!' he said. 'Mukhtar. Sabri was with you that night!'

Mukhtar, the older one, stopped.

'He was,' he said.

'The boy needs counselling,' said Owen. 'Not a knife!'

'He has no father to give him counsel,' admitted Wajja.

'Has he no uncle?' said the truculent man, still grimacing with pain.

'Alas—' said Owen.

The Bedawin began to weaken.

'He did ride with us,' one of them said.

'Sabri was all right,' said Wajja.

'He shouldn't have spoken to us like that,' said the truculent one doggedly.

'He shouldn't,' said Owen, 'and I will speak to him quietly.'

'My father is dead,' said the boy, weeping now.

'Son, it happens,' said one of the Bedawin, not unkindly.

'You can believe them,' Owen said to the boy. 'It wasn't them. Men have told you wrongly.'

The boy stood there for a moment, his face working. Then he turned on his heel and began to walk away. He had gone a few paces when he stopped and faced them.

'I have done you wrong,' he said, jerking his head in an odd little half bow.

Then he continued on his way across the Market.

'Effendi,' said the older Bedawin, Mukhtar, quietly, 'it were well this was known in his village. For he has borne himself bravely.'

*

The Bedawin were subdued afterwards.

'It is a bad business,' one of them said to Owen.

'It will remain a bad business until I find the men who did it.'

'That it should be Sabri who was killed! A man without enemies.'

'That is what makes it hard.'

The Bedawin began to drift back to the camels. Owen went with them.

'Tell me,' he said to the man he'd just been speaking to, 'was it widely know that Sabri was going to speak to the Mamur Zapt the next day?'

'He made no secret of it,' the man said.

'Among you. But what of the others in the Market?'

The man thought.

'It wouldn't have been,' he said. 'For he returned to us at dusk and by that time the Market was closed.'

*

The ward was long and thin and very crowded. The beds had been pushed together to fit more in and there was hardly space between them to stand. Owen was shocked to see how full it was. He had heard, of course, about the flood of wounded coming in from Gallipoli but seeing the ward packed like this brought it home to him.

It was quiet at this end of the ward. The bandaged figures lay motionless. Above, the great fans turned continually, and on the walls the lizards darted and froze. There was a heavy smell of disinfectant in the air, and other smells, too, which he had not smelt since his army days on the North West Frontier, the heavy, unpleasant smell of gangrene.

The other end of the ward was more lively, though. Figures were sitting up in bed, engrossed. As he came towards them there was a clap of hands and then a great cheer. He saw that there were piles of money on the floor between the beds. People bent over and scrabbled among the money and then threw notes and coins on to neighbouring beds.

'Number Two!' a voice called out. 'Second bed on the left. Wally's. A big fat green one.'

'It's moved! It's not over Wally any more.'

'Thank Christ for that!' said someone—Wally, presumably.

'It's over Bert's!'

'All right, then. Place your bets.'

'Bets on.'

'Okay, then.'

There was a loud clap, and then, this time, cries of disappointment.

'It didn't bloody work!'

'The bastard's gone to sleep!'

Owen could see now what the game was. You waited until a lizard had got above someone's bed and then clapped your hands to scare it, and hoped that its tail would fall off on the person below.

'Well, that sod is bloody useless!' grumbled someone, throwing a coin at the wall. The lizard skittered away.

'Okay, next one.'

Mrs Cunningham came in through the door.

'Now, boys, what are you up to?'

'Hello, sweetie!'

'Got a fag, sweetie?'

'Now, boys, you know you're not…'

'She's bloody useless, too,' said someone resignedly.

They turned to Owen. He held up a placatory hand.

'It's no good asking me,' he said.

He went out through the door and along a little corridor. He found Cairns-Grant in a room at the end, slumped, exhausted in a chair, smoking a pipe.

'Need it,' he said, gesturing at the pipe. 'Been on since four.'

'I'm really sorry to come bothering you,' said Owen.

'But,' said Cairns-Grant.

'That's right. I'm going to.'

'It's that autopsy, isn't it?'

'It is.'

'Well, I've had a look at him, as you asked.'

'And?'

'Two knife wounds. Left lower back. The first was what killed him. The second was to make sure.'

'He wanted to make sure, did he?'

'He wanted to do a thorough job.'

'Were there any other wounds? I was wondering, you see, if it could have been a quarrel.'

'It wasn't a quarrel,' said Cairns-Grant. 'It was a job. And done by a real professional. Small entrance wound, strong upward thrust, little bleeding, very quick, no struggle. All over in a flash. As professional a job as I've seen,' said Cairns-Grant, 'and I've seen plenty.'

⁂

'How are you getting along with your spy?' asked Lawrence, that lunch time, at the Sporting Club.

'Okay,' said Owen.

He didn't really want to talk to the archaeologist but he had been standing alone at the bar when Owen had arrived.

'Getting anything out of him?'

'A bit.'

'You need to,' said Lawrence. 'Something's getting out to the Turks. I've got people over there, you know, and they've picked it up. They say information is being fed across.'

'I daresay.'

'No, really, this is a reliable source.'

'Look, Egypt is a neutral country. Or it would be if we let it. It's an open country, anyway. People are coming and going all the time. Of course, information is getting out. The question is how important it is.'

'This information is coming from someone pretty near the top.'

'You're sure about that?'

'Pretty sure. Going by the examples my informant gave.'

'Well, if that's true, *if* that's true, it could be important, I admit.'

'It could. And especially just now.' Lawrence bent his head closer to Owen's. 'I'm picking up a lot of signs that an attack across the Canal could come at any moment,' he said quietly. 'They've been bringing up troops. They're concentrating them in several places so I don't know where the main attack will be. But I will know, and when I do, I don't want that getting back to the Turks, so that any advantage we might gain would be lost. We need to find who's leaking and stop him. That's why I am asking about that spy of yours. Can't you get something out of him?'

'I don't think he knows anything.'

'He must know something.'

'Not about this.'

'Maybe not directly. But he must know *something*, Owen. Can't you scare it out of him?'

❦

Owen felt guilty as he made his way to Mahmoud's house that evening: first, because he had not got a real spy and everyone was presuming that he had; secondly, because he ought not to be spending on Yasmin the time that he was spending. Maybe he would be able to wrap it up that evening, or pretty soon afterwards. He hoped so.

And as he sat on the divan facing Aisha it began to seem quite likely.

'It was easier than I had expected,' said Aisha. 'She agreed to come and talk to me. She remembered me, naturally. But it wasn't that. It was Mahmoud.'

'Me?' said Mahmoud, astonished.

'She knew I had married him, of course, and she wanted to meet him.'

'I do not understand this,' said Mahmoud. 'Why did she know "of course"? Our families do not know each other.'

'Everyone in the school knew,' said Aisha, 'certainly in the senior part of it. We all talked about it. We always did when someone was getting married. It was all very exciting. You can just imagine!'

'Really?' said Mahmoud, surprised, who couldn't.

'Yes. And all the more so when they heard it was Mahmoud.'

'But why?' said Mahmoud, genuinely puzzled.

'Because he was so young and handsome.'

'Aisha—'

'Several of the girls there had fathers in the Parquet, you see,' she said to Owen, 'and they were not at all young and handsome. They were old and boring and collapsed exhausted on the divan when they got home, and no one could see why anyone would ever want to marry them. But Mahmoud—'

'Aisha, I really do not know why you are saying these things.'

'—was much more glamorous. I think they were all in love with him.'

'Aisha, really—'

'And I think Yasmin admired him especially. Because of his work for the Nationalist cause. Young and glamorous, *and* Nationalist!'

'Please, Aisha!'

'I think she had worshipped him for a long time in secret. He was her hero. So when I asked her to come and see me, she jumped at the chance. But it was not because of me, alas, it was because she wanted to meet him.'

'This is conjecture, Aisha,' said Mahmoud uncomfortably.

'And, to be fair, because I think she saw this as the great breakthrough. The Nationalist Party would take up her cause, Mahmoud would defend her—'

'Please!'

'She would become a martyr for the cause and die. Happily.'

'Aisha, I do feel you should have disabused her of these foolish ideas.'

'I tried, I tried. I pointed out that my husband was a member of the Department of Prosecutions and therefore could not appear for the defence. I said that while the Nationalist Party would be delighted by her enthusiasm, they might well wish to choose for themselves the issues they made a stand on. I could see, however, that I was not taking her with me. I even sounded old to myself!'

'She is just a foolish child!' said Mahmoud warmly.

'We-ll....'

'I do not know what her father is doing, letting her do these things!'

'I don't know that he's had a great deal to say in it so far,' said Owen.

Aisha was silent.

'So you didn't really get anywhere?'

'Well, perhaps I did. In the end. I had asked her about her family. How were they taking it, I asked? Very badly, she said. They couldn't understand it, or her, at all. Her father especially. He tried, but he and she were too far apart. She could see his point of view but he couldn't see hers. He belonged to a previous generation, she said, you know, all loyalty to the Khedive. He couldn't see that things had moved on, and that all that had failed. He was hurt when she said so. She said that she didn't want to hurt him, that she loved him, really, but that surely she had to say and do what she believed to be right? I said, yes, but it was *how* you said it that was important. And perhaps how you did it.'

She fell silent again.

'Well?' said Mahmoud.

Aisha shrugged.

'Well, then she collapsed into tears and said perhaps she hadn't said it right. Well, I said, perhaps we can work on that. So, well,' she shrugged again. 'We're going to meet once more.'

'Aisha, I think you're a marvel!' said Owen.

'Well, maybe.' She was silent. 'Maybe.'

She looked at Owen. 'I think I can persuade her,' she said, 'not to insist on going to court. Not to push things too far. But if I do, it will not be because of me but because of the love and respect she feels for her family. Egyptian girls are like that, despite what they might think. They feel very strongly for their family. The family is very important to us. More important, perhaps, than it is to English people. To go against it is hard, to hurt it—well, almost unthinkable.

'Yasmin knows that if she insists on going to court, it will hurt her father deeply. It will mean the disappointment of all the hopes he had for her. She is the clever one of the family. So her father has invested everything in her—sent her to a good school, even though she is a girl. They had hoped that she would go on to train as a teacher. She will not be able to, of course, if she is known to be in trouble with the police. It is for this reason—not because of her own hopes, I think, she would be prepared to sacrifice them, but her father's hopes—that I think she would agree to be persuaded.'

'Well, that is good,' said Mahmoud. 'That is right. She should honour her father's wishes.'

'Yes,' said Aisha, 'but I think it is right for her, too. Anyone as intelligent as she is should be looking for something more in life than just marriage. It would be good for her to take up a career—good not just for her but for Egypt.'

Mahmoud didn't say anything for a moment or two. Then he said:

'You think that, Aisha, do you?'

'Yes,' she said.

He was silent for a little while, and then said:

'Do you think that of yourself, too, Aisha?'

'I think I may think it in a few years' time,' said Aisha. 'But, just at the moment,' she said, smiling, 'I've got something else on my mind.'

Owen started to get up from the divan. Aisha put up her hand.

'Wait,' she said, 'I have something to ask you from Yasmin. She would like you to speak to her father. Before she does. She thinks that might help. She says he listens to you. She cannot think why he should listen to an Englishman. She thinks it may be because you are old, too.'

Chapter Nine

Owen's orderly came in.

'Effendi,' he said, 'that violent woman is here again.'

'Sabri's wife?'

Owen got up quickly.

'Where is she?'

'She waits below. She will not come in.'

As they went along the corridor, the orderly said:

'She is calm this morning, Effendi. But it may not last. Do not go too close to her. It could break out at any moment.'

She had her son with her.

'Salah,' she said, 'come forward.'

The boy was carrying something in his hands, a package wrapped in cloth. He bowed shyly, then offered it to Owen.

Owen unfolded the cloth. Inside was a woman's headband, a circlet of woven material with little gold coins suspended from it.

'This is beautiful!' he said. He turned it over in his hands. 'Not from round here, surely?' he said, puzzled.

'It is Senussi,' said the woman. 'Sabri brought it back.'

'He brought it back for you.' Owen tried to hand it back. 'This is too fine for me,' he said. 'He meant it for you. Keep it.'

She shook her head.

'You have a wife, I know.'

'It is a kind and generous gift. But too much.'

'It is not as much as my son's life is to me.'

He tried to persuade her to take it back but couldn't.

'It is for you,' she insisted. 'Sabri would have wanted it so. This is precious, yes. The Senussi—there were lots of Senussi this time—did not want to let him have it and he had to give gold. But not as precious as his son.'

He could only thank her.

'I shall treasure this,' he said. 'It will remind me of Sabri and his people.'

He sent for water and dates and sat down with them in the courtyard to share them.

'You must have set out early this morning,' he said.

'Not so early. Hosain lent us his donkey.'

'There are still donkeys in the village?'

The woman laughed.

'Anji—you remember Anji? The donkey barber?—was down in the village and he told Hosain that the Levantine was coming, and Hosain took his donkey out to the shrine—there is a shrine in the desert near us—and left it there. And when the Levantine came, Hosain pretended he hadn't got a donkey.'

'Well, it was useful to you this morning.'

Owen asked if he could have a private word with Salah. He led him to a place where they could sit down in the shade and said:

'Salah, your father was a man who could walk by himself and I want you to be a man like that, too. Your father did not heed what others said, nor should you. So when men say that you should resent your father's death, do not listen to them.'

He could sense the boy's demurral.

'Your father was my man, Salah, and I think now that he died on my business. It is my quarrel as well as yours, and since he died on my behalf, it is my quarrel *first*. Understand?'

'All right,' said the boy reluctantly. 'It is your quarrel first. But if you do not pursue it, or—' his face brightened—'if they kill you, then it will fall to me.'

Zeinab had received an invitation to the Princess Samira's. She was pleased about this. Samira was a friend of hers: a former friend, she had been coming to think. It was nice to know that she had not altogether been cut off, and the confidence flowed back into her.

Owen was pleased too. He had been worried about her. He had not expected it would be quite so hard for her, not really believed that she would be quite so totally shunned by her friends. He had seen its effect on her. His recent conversations with Aisha had put Aisha in his mind and he couldn't help contrasting the two. Aisha only a few months before had been a shy school girl, stunned by the poised, cosmopolitan Zeinab. She had blossomed so much since her marriage that now it was Zeinab who was the silent, awkward one.

He had been impressed by the maturity Aisha had shown over Yasmin, her ability to stand apart and see her detachedly as through the eyes of one much older and more experienced, even though she and Yasmin were in fact less than two years apart in age.

Zeinab, he couldn't help being aware, had lately drawn more and more in on herself. He and she were still close, he was sure of that, it was on the other side of her, as it were, that she was withdrawing. It was if she was developing a protective shell, something that would allow her to shrug off coldness and rejection; a necessary protective mechanism, perhaps, but one that made her a lesser person.

It was beginning to worry him and he was pleased now that something was calling her out of herself and back into the warm orbit of the circles she had been part of.

⁂

It seemed to Owen that Egypt's centre of gravity was shifting eastwards. Every morning now the Ismailiya road was blocked with people, animals, and vehicles flooding east to the Canal. Great convoys of soldiers and of the things and people necessary to support them set out across the bridge every day: as well as of people and things quite unnecessary and which were merely getting in the way. Half the city's hawkers and pedlars seemed already to have deserted the hotels; the flow of fruit and vegetables, not to mention fodder for the camels and the donkeys, was no longer into the city but out towards the camps on the Canal.

Among the marchers there were now little groups of fellahin carrying their traditional wooden picks and shovels over their shoulders. Following the meeting of the Committee the other day, the extension of the Egyptian Labour Corps had indeed been decreed, and these were the first of the new recruits. Although conscription had been announced, it would take time to implement it, and they were there less because they had been obliged than because they had been drawn by the announcement of good wages with which the Government had thoughtfully accompanied the measure.

Later groups, thought Owen, would not be so willing.

It concerned him, not just because he didn't think that the policy was the right one, but because, with all the soldiers over at the Canal, he could just see who was going to be responsible for enforcing it.

He voiced his concern at the next meeting of the Committee.

'No, no, it won't be you,' said Paul. 'The omda will provide a list and then the police will go round collecting them.'

'Like the donkeys,' said one of the officers helpfully.

'*Will* the omda provide a list, when he knows that if he does, he won't ever again be able to go out on a dark night? Will the fellahin be there when the police arrive? Will the police arrive at all? Half of them are over at the Canal, trying to keep the pedlars off the premises.'

'I think you're being unnecessarily pessimistic, Owen.'

'Yes, well, I don't think so. There won't be a soldier in the place, apart from those at the Canal. What happens if there's trouble?'

'You can put it down, surely, Owen?'

'Big trouble. Twenty villages in Minya province. Fifty in two other provinces simultaneously. Just me and Selim.'

'For Christ's sake, Owen!'

'What happens if there's an invasion?'

'*Invasion?* Bloody hell, Owen!'

'Where the hell's there going to be an invasion from? We're looking after the Canal.'

'Tripolitania.'

'Haven't you forgotten, Owen?' said one of the officers, laughing. 'The Italians are on our side!'

'The Senussi, say.'

'The Senussi!'

'Actually,' said Paul, 'Owen could have a point there. They're always causing trouble.'

'Well, hell!' said one of the officers. 'A bunch of tribesmen! When we're talking about a war!'

'They could be a big bunch,' said Lawrence, 'if they could ever get together.'

'How big?'

'Thirty thousand.'

'Thirty thousand! Well, now—'

'If they could ever get together,' said Lawrence. 'Which they can't.'

'Are there actually any signs of Senussi activity?' asked Cavendish.

'No,' said Lawrence.

'No,' Owen had to admit. Then: 'Yes.'

'Yes?'

'Possible signs.'

'Well, let's wait until the possible signs become probable, shall we?' said Cavendish, smiling. 'Meanwhile—'

⌘

Mohammed Sekhmet came to the door to greet him.

'Effendi,' he said, 'you honour us.'

'The honour is mine,' Owen returned politely, as was the custom.

He led Owen along a corridor with a tiled floor and carpeted walls. At the far end of it a woman fluttered away. A young man emerged from a room and hurried past them, hardly giving Owen a glance.

Mohammed Sekhmet sighed.

'My son,' he said. He shook his head. 'The young these days have no manners.'

They entered a room fitted out in the usual way of the Turkish-Egyptian household. At the end of the room was a low dais, on which there were some large leather cushions. Beside them was a brazier with a coffee pot warming on the coals and a low table with a brass tray and two cups. Nearby was a reading stand with a huge copy of the Koran open upon it.

'At least Yasmin is not rebelling against the Holy Word yet,' said Mohammed Sekhmet drily.

They sat down on the cushions. He was pouring Owen some coffee when the young man came back.

'Father, I must go,' he said abruptly.

Mohammed Sekhmet raised his eyebrows.

'Have you no time to greet our guest, Fahmy?' he said pointedly.

The young man bowed; reluctantly, Owen sensed.

'I cannot stay, Father,' he said to Mohammed Sekhmet. 'The hoses have to be hung out and dried. They are still wet from this morning and Yasmin fears that they could be needed again at any time.'

He jerked his head, very slightly, in Owen's direction and went out.

Mohammed Sekhmet sighed again.

'I have told him about it, but it is a thing you cannot be told. It is true, though, that there is work to be done at the fire station. We are very busy just now. It is the heat, I think. And I think that the soldiers are careless.'

'They are newcomers. They do not understand the needs of the country.'

'That is true. And what I tell my son. However, you have not come to talk about my son.'

In fact, Owen wasn't at all sure what Yasmin wanted him to tell her father. He explained where they had got to.

'Garvin Pasha is just,' said Mohammed Sekhmet. 'Severe, but just. I do not know the man from Parquet, but the Parquet is usually reasonable. As for this lady—' He shook his head. 'She seems very young to me.'

'And so, perhaps, she can speak to Yasmin,' said Owen.

'Perhaps,' said Mohammed Sekhmet doubtfully.

'They are going to meet again. And it may be that she will be able to persuade your daughter. If she does,' Owen hesitated, 'I think that, for a while at least, your hand on her should be light.'

Mohammed Sekhmet nodded.

'I do not think it has been heavy,' he said, 'but she may have seen it so.'

He seemed to be thinking.

'I would like you to meet my wife,' he said suddenly.

'I would be honoured,' said Owen, surprised.

'If it is a question of how we bear ourselves towards Yasmin, then I think it would be well if she were present.'

She came into the room so quickly that Owen suspected she *had* been present, or at any rate within hearing distance. She was veiled, of course, and in the usual veil of the Turkish-Egyptian woman, white and with no nose-pipe. He did not let his eyes linger on her, however, as this would be disrespectful, and kept them firmly fixed on the ground in front of her.

Mohammed Sekhmet went through again what Owen had just told him.

'This woman,' she said, 'the one who is talking to her: you say she was at school with Yasmin?'

'Yes. And therefore I thought Yasmin might listen to her.'

'I do not like that school.'

'It is a good school,' said Mohammed Sekhmet. 'The best.'

'It has not been good for Yasmin. It has taken her away from us. It has put the wrong ideas in her head.'

'I do not think Yasmin's ideas have come from the school,' said Owen.

He could see her hand gesture impatiently.

'The school has prepared the ground,' she said. 'It has made her think not as she ought to think. It has made her look too far.'

'Too far?'

'For a woman. A woman's life is different from a man's.'

'It is right that she should look far,' objected Mohammed Sekhmet.

'Not if she is a woman. A woman cannot look too far. You have seen how it is with her. She is unhappy, dissatisfied. And now she will never be happy. What life can she lead now? What man will have her? Already she is old. But it is not that. It is what she has become. She is not submissive. She is not respectful. She puts herself forward. What man will want a wife like that?'

'An Effendi will,' said Mohammed Sekhmet.

'One of the young Effendis at the banks? Or in the offices? The Parquet, perhaps? No, they will not look at her. I know these young Effendis. They talk much about new things but it is all talk. In the end it is not they who will choose their wife but their mother. Or their father. And what mother will wish a daughter-in-law like that? Always answering back, always questioning.'

'Someone will,' said Mohammed Sekhmet stubbornly.

'No one will. And so she will have to stay forever with us, grow old with us. She will bear no children, never have a life. It is not what I would have wished for my daughter.'

'What would you have wished?' said Mohammed Sekhmet angrily. 'That she should stay all her life in the kitchen? A girl like that? Or—no, I know what it is: you would have her back in the village, in the fields!'

'The fields, no! The village, yes. My brother would have found her a good husband. Any man would be glad to marry the niece of the Pasha's man.'

'But what sort of life would she lead? What sort of life?' demanded Mohammed Sekhmet excitedly.

'A better one than in the city. Where the young learn foolish things and talk foolish words. And not just foolish words, dangerous words: look at Fahmy, look at Yasmin. She is already in trouble with the Kadi and with the Mamur Zapt. And she is still only at school. Where will it end?'

She began to rock herself and wail in the style of the village woman.

'Enough, woman! Enough!' shouted Mohammed Sekhmet angrily. 'Leave us! You shame me, you shame your family!'

'Our family is already shamed,' she retorted. 'By the daughter you have made.'

⚭

'Effendi,' said Mohammed Sekhmet, turning to Owen apologetically after she had gone, 'what can I say?'

'Nothing needs to be said,' said Owen. 'Except that I feel for you in your difficulties.'

'There are difficulties, yes. My wife is a good woman, Effendi, but she lives in the past. Her heart is still in the village in which she grew up. Her brother is the Pasha's agent, the Pasha Ismail—'

'The Pasha Ismail?'

'Yes. His lands are not far from the city. They lie along the river. There is a village there—'

'I think I know the village.'

It would be Sabri's village.

'And I think I know her brother, too. Is it not Osman Huq?'

'It is, Effendi. And if you know the man, you know my fears. I have nothing against Osman. He has always served the Pasha truly, as his father served the Pasha's father before him, and *his* father yet again before him. Their family has always served the Pasha, and that is good. But my wife thinks it must always be so. And it is not so, Effendi. The world is changing. I have no need of my daughter to tell me that. But Osman does not see this.'

'He remains true to the old ways?'

'That is exactly it, Effendi. And what I fear is that he might not choose wisely for Yasmin. What might have been a good man in the past may not be a good man today. At least to Yasmin. She has tested the city and knows the breadth of the world. A man of the village and the life of the village would not be right for her. Osman takes his thoughts from the Pasha and expects the village to take their thoughts from him. He will expect Yasmin to take her thoughts from her husband. But, Effendi, you have seen Yasmin and you know that she will not. And what then, Effendi, what then?'

'The path you originally chose for Yasmin was the right one for her. We must see she stays on it.'

'But what if she will not, Effendi? These are difficult times for families like ours, Osman's and mine. The war presses questions. It is a long time since we came with the Pashas from Turkey and we have forgotten we were Turks. But if the Turks come here, will not that remind us? A family like mine is pulled all ways at a time like this.

'In the past we had our loyalty to the Pashas and to the Khedive to guide us. But the world of the Pashas is gone and the Khedive—well, he is not the Khedive as he was. It is the British now.

'But is that right? Yasmin says it is not. But what, then, is right? We do not know in which direction to turn. I say: trust in God. My children say: what shall we do?'

When Owen got home, Zeinab was sitting out on the balcony with a drink in her hand. He showered, collected a drink himself, and went out. He could see at once that something had gone wrong.

'What's happened?' he said.

'I went to Samira's.' She shrugged. 'It was bad.'

'They froze you out?'

'No, no. They welcomed me in. But it was like going into a trap. I felt that it had all been, well, arranged. For my benefit. There were a lot of people there I didn't know. Samira's relatives. Well, I thought I knew her relatives, on my side of the family at least. But this was on the other side, Hussein's side. When he became Sultan suddenly all that side of the family became important, to Samira, anyway. I didn't know any of them. I couldn't see why I was there. But then I saw.'

She grimaced.

'Faruq came in. He came late, and as soon as he came through the door I knew what this was all about. He made straight for me and the people I was talking to somehow dropped away. After a while he said he'd like to show me his apartments at the Palace. I said, no thanks. He took me by the arm and tried to pull me away but Daoud—you remember Daoud? He's Samira's half-brother, and I've always got on with him—said: 'No, Faruq!' and he had to let me go.

'He was angry. I could tell it from the way he looked at Daoud, but Daoud stood his ground. I don't think he likes Faruq, or maybe it's just that he likes me. Anyway, Faruq hung around for a while. He kept looking at me. Then he came across. "One day I'm not going to ask," he said. "I'm going to tell." I suppose he meant when he becomes Sultan.'

'If he becomes Sultan,' said Owen.

'They all think he will. He thinks he will.'

'We'll see.'

'Anyway,' said Zeinab, 'after a while he left, and that was a relief. But then they all started on me. Samira was first. "What's wrong with you, Zeinab?" she said. "He's interested in you. Can't you be interested in him? Just a little?" "No," I said. "Not even if I wasn't married." "Don't be stupid!" she said. "You've backed the wrong horse. You've got a chance now to put that right. The Turks are going to win, and then where will you be?"'

'Let them win first,' said Owen, 'and then they can do the talking.'

'They all think the Turks are going to win. They say they're going to invade at any moment. They seem to know all about it, where the Turkish soldiers are, who their generals are, that sort of thing.'

'Do they know about the British too?'

'Of course. Well, you know Cairo.'

'They could be wrong, you know.'

'I know. But they seemed very confident. All the talk was about what was going to happen afterwards. They think the Turks will keep Hussein on the throne for a bit, but he's old and not at all well, and they think that soon Faruq will replace him. "Now's your chance, Zeinab," they said. "Get in on the right side!"'

'The right side!' said Owen.

'Well, it is the right side to them. They are Turkish, after all. *We* are Turkish. In fact,' said Zeinab, ironically, 'suddenly *everyone's* Turkish!'

They both laughed.

'Prematurely, I think,' said Owen.

Zeinab sobered up.

'But it wasn't very nice,' she said. 'They were all on to me. I said: "Why are you doing this? Why go to all this bother? Aren't there plenty of other women for Faruq?" But I know why. I'm the one he fancies just at the moment, and they think that if they help him to get me, then he'll remember it when the time comes. The bastards!'

'They're positioning themselves for when the Turks come,' said Owen. 'Or so they think.'

'Well, I don't mind that,' said Zeinab. 'That's sensible. It's the doing it at my expense that I mind. The ganging up on me. These are my own relatives, distant, I'll admit, but part of my world. And Samira is a friend! Or so I thought. She's the one I turned to when I wanted to talk things over. We used to meet all the time. And now she does this to me!'

'Maybe Faruq asked her.'

'But why did she have to agree?'

'For the same reason as the others. She wanted to be on the right side when the time came.'

'I thought she was my friend. I thought maybe she was feeling sorry for me, that she wanted to help. But to do this!'

She looked at Owen.

'It hurts worse, you know, than being frozen out.'

She put her glass down.

'But, do you know,' she said, almost in surprise at herself, 'I'm already beginning to feel better? And that is because I'm not just feeling hurt: I'm beginning to feel angry.'

Chapter Ten

'She is a foolish girl!' said Mahmoud, as he led Owen upstairs to the mandar'ah, the big reception room.

'Very young, certainly.'

'Not just young; foolish,' said Mahmoud severely.

Owen began to wonder what Yasmin had done.

'*Very* foolish,' said Mahmoud, as they went in at the door. 'Her father ought to do something about her.'

Aisha, too, seemed a little ruffled. She had seen Yasmin that morning, and Owen had been invited round so that she could report.

'Is Yasmin being difficult?' said Owen, his heart sinking.

'Yes,' said Mahmoud.

'Yes,' said Aisha, less definitely.

'You have not been able to persuade her? She won't go along with it?'

'Oh, she'll go along with it,' said Aisha. 'It took some time to persuade her but in the end she agreed. She is prepared to be let off with a warning. At one stage she seemed to be wishing that it be accompanied by a personal apology from the Mamur Zapt but I managed to convince her that wasn't necessary.'

'Aisha, you're wonderful!'

'Ye-es,' said Aisha, doubtfully.

'She has agreed?'

'Yes.'

'Then——?'

'She is a very foolish girl!' said Mahmoud.

'What exactly is the trouble?'

There was a long silence, while Mahmoud looked at Aisha and Aisha looked at Mahmoud.

'It is her attitude,' said Mahmoud.

'Well, I know that she is sometimes——'

'And her ideas.'

'Well, yes, they certainly——'

'She is lacking in respect.'

'The fact is,' said Aisha, 'she hasn't any common sense at all.'

'Well, I'm very sorry to hear——'

'She asked to see me,' said Mahmoud.

'You?'

'I said that I thought it was unnecessary,' said Mahmoud, looking severely at Aisha. 'But Aisha said it was part of the agreement.'

'That she should see you?'

'Alone,' said Mahmoud.

'Alone?'

'I said that was quite improper, and that Aisha should be there. Or perhaps my mother. Or perhaps her mother. But she insisted.'

'It was part of the agreement,' said Aisha unhappily.

'So in the end I agreed. Foolishly and wrongly.'

'What happened?'

'It was very embarrassing.'

He stopped. He seemed unwilling to say more. Owen looked at Aisha.

'She told him how much she admired him,' said Aisha.

'Loved,' said Mahmoud. 'Loved, not admired.'

'She had—admired him ever since she had read a report in the newspaper about a speech he had made at a Nationalist meeting. In it he had said everything that she believed in. She had cut the report out and hung it in her copy of the Koran——'

'Well, this is wrong,' said Mahmoud fiercely. 'This is wrong, too. She should not have kept it in the Koran. The Koran is a

Holy Book. My words are secular, profane. It is wrong to put them together.'

'—and has returned to it ever since,' continued Aisha. 'She has followed his career and read everything about him that she could. Even the Law Reports. And then when she heard he was to marry me—well, first her heart was broken, but then she was in ecstasy, for she thought it might be a chance of meeting him. She cultivated my acquaintance—I'm sorry to say I missed this—but it was difficult because I was senior to her. She thought she would never get anywhere. And then this opportunity came along.'

'Opportunity!' said Mahmoud. 'It is—is *brazen!*'

'All she wanted to do,' said Aisha, 'was tell you how much she loved you.'

'That is what I object to,' said Mahmoud. 'It is quite improper.'

'She didn't want anything more. She just wanted you to know that she loved you. She didn't expect anything in return, she knew you were already married and would be true to me—'

'Aisha, I do not think we need to continue with this. She is a very foolish girl.'

'Yes, but I don't think you should have said so. Nor quite like that.'

'You should not be defending her, Aisha. She has behaved quite improperly. Immodestly. And you, of all people, my wife—'

'Aisha is being generous,' said Owen hurriedly, 'to a very young girl—'

'Her father should reprove her. This is no way for a young woman to behave.'

Mahmoud, puritanical even by Muslim standards, naturally shy with women, and, despite his zeal for modernising and reform, deeply traditional, was very shocked. It took Owen some time to calm him down. Aisha, meanwhile, remained silent.

⌘

Once Cavendish had declared the meeting closed, everyone made for the steps leading out into the garden. It had been a long session and by the time it had ended, the heat in the room had risen to intolerable levels. The fans were merely blowing it round and round the room and eventually they had decided to switch them off. After that they had just sweated and sweltered. From time to time fresh jugs of iced water had been brought but moisture dripped out of their bodies faster than it was poured in. Sweat dripped on to the papers and made them sodden. It discoloured the smart tunics of the officers and wetted the chairs behind the knees. It prickled the eyes and made everybody irritable. So when Cavendish at last signalled 'Time' they all thankfully left their papers and headed for air.

It was midday by this time and the heat lay heavily in the garden. Through the trees the Nile sparkled blindingly in the sun but beneath their branches it was cool and peaceful. The bustle of the city seemed far away, its hubbub reduced to a background hum, against which it was just possible to make out the bells of the electric trains and, now, the more insistent clanging of a fire engine going north.

Suffragis, anticipating the general preference, brought out trays of whisky-sodas stiff with ice.

'Jesus!' said one of the officers, fanning himself. 'Another hour of that would have done me!'

'I'm off to the Canal this afternoon,' said another of the officers. 'What the hell will it be like there?'

'Hotter in the desert,' said Lawrence.

It was an innocuous remark but after the ordeal of the committee room it jarred. It had somehow the air of a put-down: as Lawrence's remarks often did.

'Very probably,' said Owen. 'And that's why I'm glad I'm not going there.'

'Not even your desert?' said Lawrence maliciously. 'To look for Senussi? If there are any.'

It drew a laugh from two of the officers.

Owen was irritated.

'They are there,' he said. 'The question is what they're doing there. And how many of them there are.'

'Well, tell us when you find out,' said the senior officer.

They all laughed. Owen turned away.

He fell into conversation with Beevor, the other archaeologist, or ex-archaeologist as Owen supposed he was now. He was older than Lawrence and less bumptious and Owen could get along with him better.

Beevor glanced at his watch.

'I must get back,' he said. 'I don't like being out of the office now, with the attack so imminent.'

It had hung over them all morning, a constant background assumption, colouring anything they talked about or did. It was affecting them all, making them all jumpy.

Lawrence came up again. He couldn't seem to leave Owen alone. Maybe that was his form of the general edginess.

'Any progress,' he asked, 'with your spy?'

'Some.'

'There needs to be. I've just heard about another leakage.'

'What's that?' said Cavendish, joining them.

'I was just telling Owen. There's a real problem with his security arrangements. My informants on the other side have just told me of another leakage.'

'Place leaks like a sieve,' said one of the officers.

'You're going to have to pick up some of these spy Johnnies, Owen,' said the senior officer.

They seemed to be all on to him this morning. Suddenly he thought that this was how it must have been for Zeinab. Perhaps it was that thought, or maybe it was just the heat and the general tension, that made him snap back.

'Are you sure that's the problem?' he said belligerently.

'I don't quite—?'

'The spy Johnnies. Are you sure that's where the information is coming from?'

'Well, where the hell else is it coming from?'

'There was a meeting the other evening. Pashas, mostly. I had an informant there.' Lawrence wasn't the only one who could have informants. 'They spent the whole evening talking about group dispositions. Turkish, largely, but British too. Very knowledgeably.'

'Well, doesn't that just prove—?'

'Wait a minute.' He turned to Lawrence. 'You've been getting information in, right? And, no doubt, making reports. Who sees the reports?'

'I bloody do,' said the senior officer.

'And—'

'Well, H.Q., of course—'

'Look, Owen, if you're suggesting—'

'Don't be ridiculous, Owen!'

'We've got security arrangements,' said the senior officer. 'Even if you haven't!'

'Hold on a moment!' said Cavendish. He turned to Lawrence. 'The information that's been getting across is top level, as I understand it?'

Lawrence nodded.

'That's right,' he said.

'The sort of information that would be at Headquarters?'

'Yes,' said Lawrence. 'But that only means that there must be a spy—'

'Does it?' said Owen. 'Who else is on the circulation list? Apart from H.Q., I mean?'

'Well—'

'The Sultan's office?'

'Got to keep him informed,' said the senior officer. 'Damn it, it's his country.'

'I think I see what Owen is getting at,' said Cavendish.

It might even be true, thought Owen.

⁕

As he and Paul were leaving, one of the officers fell in beside them.

'Damned disturbing, Owen!'

'Place leaks like a sieve!' snapped Owen.

'No, no, I don't mean that. Well, yes, it does. Probably. Got to see to it. But, no, that wasn't what I meant. It's these damned Pashas. Damned security risk. What I was wondering was, can't you just lock them up?'

'No,' said Paul. 'They rule the country.'

'Yes, I know. But that's in theory—'

'To lock them up would be foolish,' said Paul. 'It would set the whole country against us. They may not love the pashas but they wouldn't take kindly to us locking them up. No,' said Paul, 'we've got to do it a different way.'

∞

'Paul,' said Owen, after the officer had left them, 'what would that different way be?'

'Well, you know. Keep them on our side. By massaging them in the right way.'

Owen was silent for a moment. Then he said:

'Paul, Zeinab was at a party this week.'

'Oh, yes?'

'It seemed to have been laid on for Faruq's benefit.'

'Oh, yes?'

'Yes. With Zeinab as the main attraction. Prize, you might say.'

'Really?' said Paul cautiously.

'Yes. I'm not sure I like it.'

'Zeinab can look after herself.'

'Up to a point.'

'You'll just have to see it doesn't go beyond that point.'

'Paul, this is Zeinab. My wife.'

Paul was silent. Then he said:

'It needn't actually come to anything. But as long as he thinks it could come to something, he'll stay here. And this is where we want him: in Cairo and not in some place where others might get to him.'

'Yes, but she's my wife.'

'All she's got to do is keep him dangling. And any woman in Cairo can keep a man like Faruq dangling.'

'Why don't you get some other woman to do it, then?'

'Because he's taken a fancy to Zeinab. And not to someone else. Look, I know she's your wife. If I thought any harm would come to her, I wouldn't contemplate this for a moment.

But it's the way things have turned out, and from my point of view they've turned out fortunately. Zeinab is a mature woman and she'll be able to see that it doesn't come to anything. And meanwhile Faruq stays here. Where we can keep an eye on him. Otherwise he'd be off to the Riviera.'

'I'm just telling you that I don't like it.'

'Look, all she's got to do is carry on what she's doing.'

'She's not doing anything.'

'That's fine, then.'

'It's just that he keeps coming.'

'Tell her to keep fending him off, but not too irrevocably.'

'I'm not telling her that!'

'Just keep on doing as she is doing.'

'Paul, he's next in line to the throne. Do you know what he said? He said: "I'm asking now; later I'll tell."'

'He'll tell nobody. We're the ones who do the telling. And later he'll have moved on to someone else, anyway. He doesn't stay with a woman for long.'

'Yes, but meanwhile—'

⁓

He was a bent old man in a white, short-skirted galabeah, with the skirts tucked up to reveal thin, bird-like legs burnt black by the sun. He fingered the cotton carefully, almost lovingly, pulling the individual hairs out of the ball and smoothing each one gently between forefinger and thumb.

'Afifi,' he said.

'Afifi? What's that?'

'It's the kind of cotton,' said Nikos. 'There are three main kinds in Egypt. Afifi is one. The others are "Jannovitch" and "Abassi," running from brown to white.'

'Brown. Okay, so this is afifi. Does that help?'

'Not much,' said Georgiades. He'd brought the sample in that morning. 'It's all afifi from here to the Delta.'

'But it's not all the same,' said Nikos. 'It varies in stiffness and smoothness—the silkiness of the feel—and also in length of thread and in the twist of the spiral. And in about a dozen

other things. To a man like Zaghlul, here, the differences stand
out a mile.'

'Can he tell where it comes from?'

'That,' said Nikos, 'is the question.'

Zaghlul took up another ball and broke it open. This time
he sniffed it and tasted it. He took one of the lint hairs and
stretched it, testing it for tension.

He did this with several others of the balls Georgiades had
brought. Then he laid several of the hairs in a line on Nikos' desk
and stood looking down at them, nodding thoughtfully.

'Well?'

The old man picked up one of the threads, then laid it down
again.

'Not Delta,' he said.

He shook his head.

'Definitely not Delta,' he said. 'With the Delta, you can taste
the dampness. And smell the sea.'

He picked up another thread, and then a group of them, held
them together and sniffed.

'Drier,' he said. 'You smell earth.'

He sniffed again, then looked at some of the unopened balls
and then touched them delicately.

'But what earth?' he said to himself, frowning.

He went back to the sample Georgiades had brought, bundled
it all together and then raised it to his face, pushing his face into
it, looking, smelling, tasting, feeling, but now all together.

His face cleared.

'There are three estates,' he said. 'They lie along the river.
One belongs to the Pasha Selim Rokani, the other to the Pasha
Ismail, the last to the Pasha Abd es Salah Maher. It comes from
one of them.'

'If we brought you a sample from each,' said Owen, 'could
you match it with this?'

'The fields lie next to each other. The pollen drifts across,
so it would be hard. But bring me not one sample from each

but four samples, from different parts of the estates, and then perhaps I can tell you.'

'Let it be so,' said Owen. 'And tell your clients,' he said to Georgiades, 'that you can proceed.'

'That you are ready to proceed,' amended Nikos. 'That gives us time to make suitable arrangements.'

Mrs Sekhmet, forgetting all propriety, spoke first.

'Effendi,' she pleaded, 'set not your face against her!'

'Effendi,' said Mohammed Sekhmet, 'if you were now to wash your hands of her I would understand. Nevertheless—'

'She is young,' broke in Madame Sekhmet, 'and foolish—'

'What has she done now?' said Owen resignedly.

'Nothing!' cried Madam Sekhmet. 'Yet they have arrested her!'

'She *has* done something,' said Mohammed Sekhmet. He sounded defeated. 'But now she must abide by the consequences.'

'Where is she?'

'In the Bab-el-Khalk. One told us and we came running, but she had already been delivered.'

'And so, in our distress, we turn to you!'

'Again!' Mohammed Sekhmet shook his head. 'Wife, this cannot go on!'

Owen sent to the door and told Nikos to have the girl brought.

'Do you want the policemen, too?' asked Nikos, getting up from his desk.

'Might as well. Then we can hear both sides.'

There was, however, only one side. Yasmin denied nothing. She accepted that she had chained herself to the Abdin Palace railings.

'Like the British women?' said Owen, remembering the end of their previous encounter.

'We can learn from our enemies,' said Yasmin.

Mohammed Sekhmet groaned.

'Why did you chain yourself to the railings?'

'To protest.'

'I'm sure of that. But over what particularly?'

'Conscription,' said Yasmin. 'Conscripting Egyptian men to fight in the British Army.'

'They're not exactly going to fight. It's into the Labour Corps.'

'It's as good as fighting. They're going to dig trenches which will be used against their brothers.'

'Yasmin, you know nothing of this. Be silent!' ordered her mother.

'How can I be silent?' demanded Yasmin. 'When I see injustice being done?'

'Injustice is always being done,' said Madame Sekhmet, 'and it is not for us to try and alter it.'

'That is not so, Mother,' said Yasmin defiantly. 'And it is not,' with a touch of glee, 'what my father has taught me!'

'I?' cried Mohammed Sekhmet.

'Certainly,' said Yasmin. 'Have you not always told me that I must stand up for what is right?'

'Yes, but not like this!'

'All right, all right,' said Owen hurriedly. 'Now let's get straight what actually happened.'

He looked at the police officers. They were the same two as before.

'Well, Effendi, it was like this. Abou and I were just walking across Abdin Square, and had stepped aside—yes, Abou?'

'It was very hot.'

'Yes, thank you, Abou. And we stepped aside for a moment to talk to the men at the Palace Gate. And one of the guards came up and said. "That bloody girl is back." And I said: "Oh, ho, she's up to her tricks again, is she?" And he said: "No chance of anything like that, mate; she's chained herself to the bloody railings." So Abou and I went along to see.

'And I said: "You can't do that sort of thing here." And she said, "Why not?" And I said, of course she couldn't do that here, it stood to reason she couldn't.'

'Breaking the law.'

'Yes, thank you, Abou. I told her she was breaking the law. "What law?" she said. Well, Effendi, at the time I couldn't for the life of me think which law. So I said: "Never mind that. You'd better come along with me." And she said: "Certainly, officer." And I said: "All right, come along, then." And she said: "I can't." And I said: "Why the hell not?" And she said: "Because I'm chained to the railings, you dumb oaf."'

'Yasmin!'

'And I said: "Right, I've got it now. I'm charging you with being abusive to an officer of the law in pursuit of his duties." "Okay," she said. "Fine." "Where's the key?" I said. "Here," she said, and showed it me. Before dropping it down the front of her burka.'

'Yasmin!'

'And I said to Abou: "If we don't watch out, we're going to land ourselves in the shit. What are we going to do?" and Abou said—'

'Land somebody else in it instead.'

'Thank you, Abou. Those were wise words. So we sent to the Bab-el-Khalk—'

'And eventually,' said Yasmin impatiently, 'that strange Englishman came. McPhee, or whatever his name is. And I will say this for him: he was polite—he called me Miss—and he listened to me. He asked me what was the point I was trying to make, and when I told him, he said: "You know, I can get a woman to search you for the key. Or I can get a blacksmith to file through the chain. Or you can find the key yourself and unlock your chains. Would it not make the point equally well if you did that and I promised to take you to the police station and charge you with causing a breach of the public peace?" And I said: "Well, I'm not happy with being charged with a breach of the peace, because peace is exactly what I'm doing this for; but if you can think of some other charge, I will come with you." So,' said Yasmin proudly, defiantly, and—looking at her father—a little apprehensively, 'here I am.'

'I had thought we were getting somewhere,' said Owen.

'We were. But that was in the light of the status quo. Since then you've changed everything.'

'Changed everything?'

'By bringing in this new law. Conscripting people.'

'Yasmin, this is not for you—'

'But it *is*, Mother!' Yasmin faced her. Can't you see? Someone must protest. It won't be the fellahin. And yet they're the ones who will be hurt. They're the ones who are going to be digging these trenches, probably while everyone is shooting at them. But they'll say nothing, they never say anything— So someone else must do it for them.'

'There are plenty of people speaking on their behalf, you know, Yasmin,' said Owen.

'And getting nowhere,' said Yasmin. 'But if *I* do it—a mere girl—won't that attract attention!'

'You have attracted enough attention,' said Mohammed Sekhmet sternly. 'Now there must be a stop to it.' He turned to Owen. 'Effendi,' he said, 'we have troubled you too long. You have tried to help, and for that we thank you. But enough is enough. If that is what she wills, then let it go to the court. In the end, God alone decides. But meanwhile, Effendi, I will see that she troubles you no more. Yasmin, you will go to your uncle in the country. You wished to speak for the fellahin; now you will get to know the fellahin. And it may be that you will find they are not as you thought.'

⁕

Zeinab had attended her first lectures at the university—yes, she had been able to fix it—and came home looking thoughtful. Owen thought that this might be a natural outcome of studying ethics and was impressed. She sat silently out on the balcony and he didn't like to disturb her, merely putting a glass by her hand. From down below in the square the occasional cry of an arabeah driver floated up—it was a more peaceful square than the Ataba—together with the murmurs of the old woman selling oranges from her green pyramid of cannon balls beneath the trees; and from somewhere far off in the hot, dusty streets of the Old City came the familiar faint clanging of a fire engine's bell.

'I met Latifa today,' Zeinab said suddenly.

'Oh, yes?'

'Yes. She was giving one of the other lecture courses.'

'A talented lady.'

'Yes. I find her more and more interesting. As a person, you know. At first I didn't. She is older than me, of course, and her world was so different from mine—you know, the hospital, and all that charity work. It all seemed so—so earnest. Rather joyless, I felt, although I believe that now to be wrong. And she herself seemed so single-minded, so committed to her causes. It rather put one off, put me off at any rate. I always felt guilty when I was with her. So I rather tended to steer clear of her.

'But, lately, you know, I have been thinking about her quite a lot—the way she has managed to make a life for herself. Despite everything. I told myself at first that it was easier for her because she was a widow and that she had been able to draw on her husband's position. But I think it must still have been very difficult for her, after her husband died. She had to make her way alone. And I think she has done it so successfully.'

'I've always warmed to her, myself,' said Owen. 'Though I know what you mean. She does rather button-hole you.'

'Button-hole?' said Zeinab, to whom the expression was new. He mimicked it, and she laughed. 'Yes,' she said, 'that is what she does. "Button-hole." This afternoon she button-holed me.'

'She did?'

'She asked me what course I was doing, and when I told her, she said: "Zeinab, why are you doing a course like that? It is so beside the point. It is not what Egypt needs, or what you need." I said: "What other course is there?" And she said: "Mine!" And I said: "Not for me, thanks. I don't know anything about children." And she laughed and said: "You will, Zeinab. You will." "And anyway," I said, "I'm not sure that I want to know. I want to keep away from anything like that. It's another of those things that shut you up in a cupboard. Not for me, thanks."

'And she said: "Zeinab, my darling, this is where it all starts. It's where cupboards start—the way we bring up our children. And if we want to break open the cupboards, this is where we must begin." Well, I must say, I had never thought of it like that. It took me aback. But still I said I wasn't interested. "It's too private," I said, "too inward-looking. The family is what I want to get away from. Especially my family." "Not my course," she said. "It's for administrators, women who will work in Health Departments and hospitals, setting up projects. It's just the thing for you." 'Anyway,' said Zeinab, almost defiantly, 'she's going to tell me more about it. And I'm switching to her course.'

༻∘༺

The next morning when Owen got into his office, Nikos said that Garvin wanted to see him. McPhee was already in there and so was a very worried-looking Mohammed Sekhmet.

'Owen,' said Garvin, 'there have been a lot of fires lately.'

'Yes, I've been thinking that myself. It's the heat, I suppose—'

'Mohammed thinks they're not being started accidentally.'

Chapter Eleven

'Effendis,' said Mohammed Sekhmet, 'there have been more fires than usual lately, and at the Fire Station we have been asking why this should be. At first we thought it must be the heat: but then we noticed that many of the fires were at liquor houses and we thought they could be due to the foolishness of the soldiers. For, Effendis, it is mostly the soldiers who use them. And some of my men were angry, saying that these men descended on us like locusts and despoiled the land; that before they came, liquor houses were few and there were few fires. And they blamed the fires on the foolishness of the men, saying that they got drunk, and that while they were drinking, they were smoking, and that, in the foolishness of alcohol, they threw their cigarettes away and cared not where they fell. That is what they said, Effendis,' said Mohammed Sekhmet apologetically.

'And probably not unjustly,' said Owen.

'And, you see, there are so many of these liquor houses these days. They have sprung up like flowers in the desert after rain. And, with so many soldiers in the city, they are always full. We thought at first that when the soldiers went away everything would go back to being as it had been; but when the soldiers went away, more soldiers came. And there are now the wounded as well. It is not for me, Effendis, to speak ill against men who have been in the shadow of death, but it cannot be denied that some of them now take death, as life, lightly. Or so my men murmured, Effendis, and some of them become hot against the foreign soldiers, saying that this came about because of their impiety and sinfulness, and through their not following the laws of the Prophet.'

Mohammed Sekhmet paused.

'I do but say what they said, Effendis.'

'That is understood,' said Garvin.

'I reasoned with them,' said Mohammed Sekhmet, 'saying that men always blamed the stranger; but in my heart I could not but agree with them. "It is the vengeance of God," they said. "Why should we seek to stay God's wrath?" And I said: "It is not for us to assess God's purposes. All that we can do is our duty." Well, they agreed with that, although still they murmured.'

Mohammed Sekhmet paused again. He looked older, and the energy and drive which had so impressed Owen when he had first seen him, in action at the fire, seemed to have drained out of him.

'We understand the load you carry,' Garvin said sympathetically.

Mohammed Sekhmet bowed in acknowledgement.

'That is what the job is,' he said, 'and I do not complain. Nor would I have come to you, but for—'

He sighed.

'Effendis, I am growing old and perhaps careless. I do not see things as I used to. I did not see this. It was Yussef who saw it and brought it to my attention.'

'What did he see?'

'We were very quick to get to a fire last week. It was in the early morning and the streets were empty, so I said: "Let us try our new motorised fire engine." And with it we sped through the streets and arrived before the fire had time to take a hold. And I said: "Thanks be to God!" and would have left it at that.

'But Yussef, going through the building afterwards to make sure all was safe, saw where a pile of materials had been brought together, and spirits emptied over them, and smelt paraffin. "Brothers, there is ill-doing here," he said.

'Well, we talked about it, and agreed that the next time we were called out we would look to see if there were signs that the fire had not happened by chance. But when the next time came, we were slow getting to it—we had not the motorised engine that time—and all was burned to the ground, and although we looked, we could see nothing untoward.

'But Yussef was not content and enquired of the people round about, and one of them had seen a man running from the back of the liquor store just before it burst into flames. And Yussef followed the path of this man—it was among the rubbish of a bath house—and found an empty can smelling freshly of paraffin.'

Owen went to the site later. The liquor house was beside a hammam, a public bath-house, and the hammam was beside a rubbish dump, from where it drew its fuel. Owen, wisely, had never studied such a dump before. The rubbish came from all over the city and was piled feet high on a deserted building plot behind the bath-house. For the most part it was household waste, green leaves, vegetable peelings, the offal of poultry or rabbits, rags, broken pots, discarded divans, and general excrement.

Above it the air was dense with flies; and when you looked down, especially on the moist, organic matter, the rubbish was not just black with flies, it was seething with them and other insects. Everything seemed alive. He was looking at a small hammock covered with green slime. Suddenly it heaved itself up and he saw to his astonishment that it was a cat. There were similar hummocks all over the place and similar cats, dozens of them. They prowled round the rubbish and made their way on to the top of the bath-house, where they warmed themselves beside the ventilation.

There were paths through the rubbish, where the refuse had been pressed down and trodden on, but still the ground was squelching under foot and every step released fresh odours and fresh swarms of flies. Owen was in his boots but even so he hesitated.

Yussef, however, the fireman he had borrowed from Mohammed Sekhmet, was barefoot and he did not hesitate. He strode
ahead up one of the paths and after a moment Owen followed
him.

There were cats lying in the way but they did not move. Cats
rarely moved for people in Egypt. They had to step round them.
The cats merely lay there and watched them.

Yussef led Owen along the track to where there were the
remains of an old house, filled with rubbish inside and with
goats feeding on the rubbish in the shade of the walls. Yussef
stopped and pointed.

'Here, Effendi!'

It was where he had found the can. He had picked it up and
taken it to the fire station and Owen had seen it.

'What made you come this way?' said Owen.

'I saw something glinting in the sun and when I looked I
saw it was a can.'

The track led back to the bath-house and then on to the rear
of the liquor house, now blackened and charred.

'There was only the one path,' said Yussef.

'Not easy to see in the dark,' said Owen.

'There would have been moonlight. That was why the man
was seen.'

Owen nodded. There would have been shadows, too, the
shadow of the bath-house and occasional shadow from the
heaps of rubbish.

He walked further along the track. It rose over a mound of
rubbish and then descended on the other side towards some
houses. In this part of Cairo people lived cheek by jowl with
the rubbish. This was where the man would have run to after
he had discarded the can.

It was not here, though, that he had been seen, but further
back. Owen retraced his footsteps.

The sighting had been just at the point where the track ran
behind the bath-house, and it had been by one of the bath
attendants. The fires which heated the water for the baths were

never allowed completely to die out and the attendant, on night duty, had gone outside to collect a barrow-load of fuel. It was then that he had seen the man.

'He nearly knocked me down!' he said, aggrieved. 'I had just stepped out when, bang, he ran into me! Nearly knocked me over. And the next minute he was off, nipping in and out of the heaps like the Devil himself was after him.'

'Did you get a look at him?'

The watchman considered.

'He had a box,' he said.

'Box?'

'Can,' McPhee said later. 'The one that was found. And it had been bought that evening from a local shop.'

'Does the shopkeeper remember who bought it?'

'Vaguely. An effendi, he says, but I don't think he means that. He just means that the man wasn't wearing a galabeah. The attendant at the bath-house says that, too. Trousers, a jacket. Some sort of uniform perhaps. Similarly dressed, anyway. The shopkeeper had seen him hanging around earlier in the day. But he doesn't remember him very clearly.'

'See if you can find someone else who does,' said Owen.

The scenes of the fires remained disturbingly with him. Both houses, or the remains of both houses, still reeked of alcohol but in the second, the one next to the bath-house, Owen had fancied he could pick up the smell of paraffin.

The first house was less damaged than the second. The fire, as Mohammed Sekhmet had said, had not had time to take hold and while most of the contents had been burned, the walls were standing.

In a back room was a pile of odd things that had been deliberately put together; doors from a cupboard, cloths, pieces of paper, some sacking. Nearby, on the ground, was a row of empty bottles. Their caps lay in a neat little pile to one side. The contents had obviously been poured over the materials before they had been lit.

Here in this room the fire had not taken hold but in another room, adjoining, there were traces of other objects similarly gathered in the centre of the floor and here it was only burned fragments that remained. Again there were empty bottles nearby.

There had been soldiers in both liquor houses at the time the fires had occurred, but fortunately it had been so late that most of the carousers had left.

Owen was able to track down some of them. They came from the nearest hospital.

'Went up like a rocket, mate. In a great ball of flame. We sniffed burning and were just saying, what the hell is that, when the little bloke, Ali, comes running and says, get to hell out of here, quick! And we did, too, by God, for the door went down at the end and we could see the flames. So we grabbed everybody and pulled them outside and had just about got out of the door when there was a bloody great bang and the next minute we were flat on our faces in the street.'

'Yes, mate, we had been drinking, what the hell do you think we were there for? Course we'd been smoking but we're not daft, are we, we know enough to put the fags out.'

'Yes, we were pissed, but not that pissed. Had somebody gone out the back? Mate, someone was *always* going out the back, it comes in so it's got to go out, but no one was out the back just at that moment.'

'See anyone! Mate, the way we were, we wouldn't have seen Queen Neffer-Titty if she'd walked in....'

'But I'll tell you what it was like, it was like being back at bloody Gallipoli, and I wouldn't wish that on anyone.'

The Army issued a warning that liquor houses could be the target of enemy action and ordered all ranks to be on their guard when they were in such places. All ranks took this seriously and expressed their seriousness by beating up a few inoffensive civilians who had the misfortune to be nearby.

The representatives of the Grand Mufti and of the Sultan came to see Owen again and he passed their messages on to the appropriate authorities, who expressed their regret. After due consideration, however, they felt unable to close down all liquor houses as had been requested.

'But something must be done about it, Owen,' said McPhee, perturbed. He had just been to the hospital to question the soldiers involved. Some of them were suffering from burns and all were suffering from a sense of injustice. This sort of thing was all right in the Dardanelles, they said, but not when you were having a quiet drink with your mates.

The High Commissioner pointed out to Owen that attacks on Allied soldiers were prejudicial to relationships with the civil population. Likewise vice versa, said Owen. The High Commissioner, when he had understood it, didn't take the remark kindly and suggested that Owen move the search for the arsonist up his list of priorities.

Curtis, in the bar, said that at least Owen had something to go on: the arsonist was clearly opposed to the consumption of alcohol and may have had a feeling of antagonism towards foreign soldiers. Didn't that narrow it down a bit? Yes, said Owen: to about ten million.

⁂

His thoughts turned back to Georgiades. He could really do with him on ordinary duties just now. Surprisingly, Georgiades seemed to think the same. In fact, he said, the sooner he could get back on ordinary work and out of the world of business, so much, very definitely, the better. Rosa's speculation was weighing heavily upon him.

'I think about it all the time,' he said. 'It's getting me down.'

'Well, don't show it's getting you down,' said Owen. 'Otherwise people here in the hotel will be wondering.'

'No, it's all right,' said Georgiades. 'At least from that point of view. They all think I've got a big deal in the offing. And I have,' said Georgiades, sunk in deep depression, 'I have. Only it's not the one they think.'

He had lost weight and was no longer drinking.

'Can't touch the stuff,' he said gloomily. 'Not now.'

It all added conviction. In the hotel now they were certain that he was on the brink of pulling something off.

'That Greek,' said Curtis, 'the one who is a spy: well, he's about to bring off something big.' He laid his finger alongside his nose. '*Really* big. You can tell it, you know.'

Owen was happy that such should be the general impression; and even happier that soon he would be in a position to pull Georgiades out. The middleman who had contacted Georgiades, Iskander, was in the hotel regularly now finalising details. There were mostly financial details and Owen was worried that something might go wrong. He had a financial expert from Customs standing by and Georgiades checked everything with him, nodding his head thoughtfully to all Iskander's proposals but agreeing, initially, nothing.

About the actual transferring of the cotton, nothing was said. Iskander would handle all this side. They had a pretty good idea now where the cotton would come from. Nikos had been able to match samples and had established that the cotton Georgiades had been shown had come almost certainly from the estates of the Pasha Ismail. It could, thought Owen, have been any Pasha.

The Customs and Excise men would be watching the estate closely and any action could be left to them. Nikos, meanwhile, was concentrating on Iskander.

Owen had an unexpected visitor. It was Nuri Pasha, Zeinab's father. As he came in he wrinkled his nose in a faint expression of distaste.

'Austere, dear boy, austere!' he said, looking round him at the room. 'Rather too like a barrack-room for me. But then, I suppose the Bab-el-Khalk *is* a barracks.'

'Not quite, Nuri!' protested Owen.

'All these new Ministerial buildings are. And so it is important to make one's own room a small centre of civilisation.'

'This is the other side of civilisation. The necessary underside.'

'I have always preferred the top side, myself,' said Nuri. 'Or, at least, the illusion of being on the top side. And so when I was at the Ministry I insisted on furnishing my office myself, and did so most lavishly. If we do not give people the impression of superiority, then how can we expect them to believe in us? Even though the reality, as I, alas, sadly found, may be different.'

Nuri's stay at the Ministry of Justice had been regrettably brief. He had been Under-Secretary at the time of a notorious incident, over which he had been obliged by his position to take sides. Unfortunately, he had taken the wrong side: the British side. Ever since, his political career had been blighted, although he lived in perpetual hope of its revival. 'After all,' he frequently said, 'surely loyalty will one day be requited.' That, however, was not the issue. As always in Egypt, the question was, among several possible winners, loyalty to whom?

'To what, my dear Nuri, do I owe the pleasure of your visit?' asked Owen, sending for coffee.

'Concern for Zeinab.'

'Ah!' said Owen, thinking that news of Zeinab's difficulties must have reached him. 'It is true,' he said, 'that she has been having rather a hard time lately.'

'To be expected, dear boy. To be expected!'

'Well, perhaps it is. But I was sad to see it. There's no need for her to cut herself off. Or to be cut off.'

'Quite so!'

'She does feel it.'

'I'm sure, dear boy, I'm sure!'

'Some of the blame, no doubt, lies on her side—'

'She always was intransigent, dear boy.'

'But I do feel that the way her family and friends have shut her out—'

'Not her family. I can assure you. At least, not her father.'

'But her family at large—'

'Millstones, dear boy, I have always felt them to be like millstones. Hanging round your neck.'

'Could they be persuaded, do you think, to take—?'

'A more civilised view? I think they could. And should,' said Nuri firmly.

This was going rather well. If Nuri really was prepared to do some work on the family—

'I said as much to Samira only this morning.'

'Yes, well, Samira—'

'Wishes Zeinab nothing but good, I assure you.'

'Well, I know, but—'

'I am afraid that Zeinab left with the wrong impression after that gathering the other night.'

'You think so?'

'I'm sure of it. Faruq is really a very agreeable fellow—'

'Wait a minute....'

'One must build bridges. Bridges to the future.'

'Bridges to the future?'

'Well, you know, dear fellow, with the Turks only on the other side of the Canal—'

 formation

Owen knew only too well. Nuri, like the other Pashas, was hedging his bets. But surely not at the expense of his daughter?

'Nuri, I don't think she cares for him, you know.'

'But surely that can be altered?'

'Nuri, she is my wife!'

'Well, yes, but—'

He could see it all now. Zeinab would be the bridge by which the family secured its interest. Either way. Whether the Turks came or not. If the Turks came, then they were obviously banking on Faruq's pro-Turkish sympathies being rewarded, opening up benefits to those he favoured. But even if they didn't come, Faruq still had every chance of the succession, and the benefit might still come flowing.

It was the age-old trick, in England as in Egypt, wherever there were monarchs: get your woman into the king's favour and so tilt the cornucopia in your direction. Nuri's ancestors had practised it for centuries, and now Nuri was doing exactly the same.

'One must be civilised,' said Nuri.

'Sabri?' said the man at the bank. He hunted through the ledgers. 'Yes, he does have an account here.'

'Did, I think,' said Owen. 'Can you tell me anything about him?'

'As it happens, I can,' said the man. 'And that is because he made such a nuisance of himself the first time he came here. And, indeed, every other time, but now we've got used to it.'

'Nuisance?' said Owen.

The man shrugged.

'Well, you know these simple villagers,' he said. 'They get a fixed idea about something and after that you can't unfix it. This Sabri, for instance: I mean, he's just a simple villager,' said the banker, a man of the city, an occupier of an office and wearer of a tarboosh, a Copt, like Nikos, and therefore not simple at all. 'He shouldn't be using a bank like ours. But he insisted on it. He came in one day and said he wanted to see the boss. "Boss," he said, "I'm handing over to you a lot of money and I want you to look after it." "Certainly," says the manager. "How much?" And when Sabri tells him he laughs and says: "That's not a lot to me, Mr Sabri. In fact, I don't know that you'd be advised to bank with us at all." But Sabri insisted. "No," he said, "I want a proper bank. Because this is going to be a proper thing." And he made such a fuss about it that in the end the manager said okay.

'But that's when the problem started. "Let's have a specimen signature," we said. "What?" said Sabri. And then it turned out he couldn't write. "I'll make a mark," he said. Now you can't have a customer making marks at a bank like ours, so we tried to tell him he'd be better off somewhere else: the village money-lender, or something. "No, thanks," he said. "You don't know our money-lender. You're the people I want."

'Well, it went on and on, but in the end we agreed. The trouble was, it happened the next time he came in. And the next. The people at the windows didn't know what to make of him. He would come in and sit himself down on the floor and when at last someone asked him what he wanted, he would say: 'I'm

Sabri,' as if that explained it all. And then whoever was dealing
with him would have to go through it all, signature, mark, that
sort of thing. So finally we got it that he always went to the same
man, Zeki, one of our oldest clerks, who didn't come all bright
and bumptious over him. In fact, he used to go out for coffee with
him. You wouldn't believe that, would you? You wouldn't believe
a manager like ours would even agree to a thing like that, would
you? But he did. Mind you, Zeki has been here with us for about
a hundred years now, and, to be frank, it doesn't make much difference if he goes out for coffee, for all the good he does here—'

'Can I have a word with Zeki?'

'Go out for coffee with him, if you like. But it's only the
pavement restaurant round the corner.'

The restaurant consisted of a large tray with the food heaped
in the middle and bread stuck on spikes around the sides. Customers sat on the ground and helped themselves, and the pro-
prietor went round with a long-sprouted coffee pot and poured
coffee into little enamel cups. It was the sort of place where Sabri
would have felt at home and Owen guessed that was why Zeki
had taken him there.

'Well, you know,' said Zeki, 'he came from the country and it
was difficult enough being in the city without all the extra fuss of
being in a bank. But he wasn't stupid. Oh, no! That's the mistake
these young effendi make in the bank. They think everyone who's
not like them is backward. But Sabri was a very intelligent man.
I used to like talking to him. You could always learn something
from him, about conditions in the village, or even further afield,
what the cotton crop would be like, you know, all that sort of
thing, which is actually quite useful to us in the bank.

'I used to go back and tell it to Mr Ventezi—he's the manager
here—and Mr Ventezi would say: "That's good information,
you pay for the coffee." But Sabri would never let me. "You are
a poor man, as I am," he would say.'

'When I got to know him, I would say: "If you are so poor,
why bring your money here?" And he would say: "It is for my
boy." He told me all about his son and his hopes for him. "He

is intelligent," he said, "and capable of great things. But for that he must go to the madrissa. Intelligence without learning is like water poured on the sand."

'One could not help warming to him. I looked forward to his coming. And in my way I tried to help him. "Sabri," I said, "this money is much to you and hard earned. But it is not much when it is set against the costs of a great madrissa. I fear it will not be enough."

'He used to go silent then. "What you must do," I told him, "is go to your Pasha. Ask him for money to send your boy to school. It is the sort of thing Pashas often do." "Not our Pasha," he said. "Our Pasha is mean and greedy and takes rather than gives." And he would not go to him.

'But this time I pressed him harder than usual. "If you will not ask him for money," he said, "ask him for his word. There are waqufs for bright boys and I can tell you where to go. But you will need support and that is where your Pasha comes in. His word could secure your son a place and money and it will cost him nothing."

'Well, at first he would not. "He doesn't like me," he said. "He knows I am not easy under his yoke." "Nevertheless, go to him," I said, "and speak mildly. For the money you have put aside for your son is not enough."'

'And did he say he would?'

'I had to reason with him for a long time. But, yes, in the end he said he would.'

Chapter Twelve

By the time Owen reached the village it was already mid-morning. The heat lay on the village in an almost palpable layer, subduing everything. A few dogs lay in the shade, their tongues lolling out. A few naked children played quietly in the shadows of the walls. In the houses women had already begun to prepare the mid-day meal and thin smoke climbed up from the yards and lay languidly in the air. The birds had mostly fallen silent. Only the doves in the lebbek trees maintained their low, continuous background purr.

Owen rode up to Sabri's house and dismounted. The boy, Salah, came out and took the horse's head.

'I will take her into the shade, Effendi,' he said, 'and give her some water. She will be ready when you need her.'

First, though, he went back into the house and returned with his mother.

'We are honoured, Effendi,' she said. 'You are most welcome.'

'The honour is mine,' said Owen.

She led him into the small courtyard and they sat down on the earth. She was unveiled and received him boldly. Behind her, though, in the doorway of the house, was another woman, and she was veiled.

There was a kettle already on the small brazier and she offered him tea.

'Salah is well?'

'Salah is well and confined to the village,' said the woman pointedly.

'Perhaps that is best. Yet here in the village there will always be foolish people ready to egg him on.'

'So?' said the woman, looking at him sharply.

'Sabri wished him to go to school in the big city.'

'He paid money for it: but it is not enough.'

'So I understand. I have been speaking to a man at the bank. However, he said there was a possibility of his being able to benefit from a waquf.' A waquf was a charitable bequest. 'All that would be necessary would be that someone should speak for him.'

'Sabri told me.'

'The man at the bank said that he had counselled Sabri to go to the Pasha and ask for his word in support.'

'Yes.'

'Did he do it?'

'He spoke to Osman Huq,' said the woman bitterly, 'and much good it did him.'

'Osman Huq? The Pasha's man?'

'The Pasha's man. We see no Pasha here. Osman is the Pasha's face.'

'And he denied his support?'

'He said that before the Pasha would do things for Sabri, Sabri must do things for the Pasha. But he had always turned his back on the Pasha, so why now should the Pasha help him? Sabri said—and it cost him much to say this, he told me after—that when the boy had been to the school, he would be able to serve the Pasha better.

'But Osman said the Pasha did not want service of that sort. What he needed was men who worked in the fields, and that was where Salah ought to be. To aim otherwise was to nourish the spirit of discontent. A similar spirit, he said, to the one that existed in his father!'

'This made Sabri angry and he said: "If you will not speak for me, there are others who will." And Osman taunted him and said:

"Not in the village, there aren't!" And Sabri said: "The Mamur Zapt will speak for me." And Osman laughed, and said: "You foolish man! Why should the Mamur Zapt speak for the likes of you?" And Sabri said: "I go to see him, and when he hears what I have to say, he will look kindly on me."'

'He told Osman that, did he?' said Owen.

The veiled figure in the doorway came out into the yard.

'Salaam Izayek,' said Owen politely.

'And to you, salaam,' returned the woman automatically.

He recognised the voice.

'What is this man doing here?' demanded Yasmin, turning to Sabri's widow.

'We have been talking about Salah,' said Sabri's widow, surprised.

'Do you know who he is?'

'He is the Mamur Zapt.'

'Then why is he here?'

'He has been good to Salah.'

'Do not trust him.'

'Yasmin, I have spoken with this man before and since Sabri's death he has helped me greatly.'

'Beware of him. He is English and his interests are not the same as ours.'

'There are interests which cut across divides,' said Owen, 'and one of them is seeing that a child gets the education that it deserves.'

'I know the kind of education that you think we deserve,' said Yasmin. 'It is the one that takes us away from our people.'

'Yasmin, you are older than Salah and have had the chance to make up your own mind. Let Salah be given that chance too.' He turned to Sabri's widow. 'The man at the bank said that he knew of a waquf that would serve. All that would be necessary was that someone should speak for Salah. If the Pasha will not, then I will. If, that is, you wish it, for I know that you have misgivings.'

'Sabri would have wished it.'

'Sabri is gone. It is for you to decide.'

'Sabri would have wished it more than anything else in the world,' she said.

'Fatima, do not listen to this man. Do not take his money.'

'It is not my money,' said Owen. 'It will come from the Ministry of Waqufs. All I will do is speak for Salah.'

'Fatima, there is no need for an Englishman to speak for Salah. I will speak to my uncle and—'

'Sabri has already spoken to him.'

'He has already spoken to him?'

'Yes. And your uncle denied him. With hot and foolish words.'

'Fatima, I am sure this is a mistake. I will speak to my uncle and—'

'Yasmin!' said a stern voice from beyond the wall.

'Come in, Osman Huq!' called Sabri's widow.

✧

Osman Huq came through the gates.

'Yasmin,' he said, 'your aunt—' He stopped, seeing Owen. 'Yasmin,' he said angrily, 'have you been talking to a man?'

'I have talked to him before.'

'That is no answer! It is improper, immodest of you!' He looked darkly at Sabri's widow. 'Have you no shame, woman, to allow—?'

'It is not her fault,' said Yasmin hastily. 'She told me to stay in the house. But when I saw who she was talking to—'

'No, Osman Huq,' said Sabri's widow, folding her arms, 'no, I have no shame. Yasmin used to come to this house as a small girl and she is welcome now as a big one. And I have no sense of shame if she hears me now speaking to a man who helped me when you would not.'

'Uncle—'

'I came about the waquf,' said Owen.

'The waquf is no concern of yours,' said Osman Huq coldly.

'Quite right, Uncle—'

'Then whose concern is it?' asked Sabri's widow. 'If it is not yours either?'

'What is right for the boy can be discussed another time.'

'Ah, but, you see, I was discussing it now.'

'Uncle, I am sure there was a mistake—'

'Be silent, girl!' He faced Owen. 'Effendi, neither the waquf, nor the boy, nor this woman here, are any concern of yours. It would be best if you left. Now.'

'Well, there, Uncle, I agree with you, but—'

'Girl, will you be quiet!' shouted Osman Huq furiously.

'But,' Yasmin continued doggedly, 'I think it was wrong of you not to give Salah your support—'

'Agree?' roared Osman Huq, goaded beyond endurance. 'Think? What do I care if you agree? What do I care what you think? A woman has no business to have thoughts. Much less a slip of a girl! A woman should have the thoughts of her husband and the sooner I get a husband for you—'

'Osman Huq,' said Sabri's widow with dignity, 'it is not for you to say who is welcome in my house. Nor to shout in my yard. I think it would be best if you left. Now.'

Osman Huq pulled himself together.

'Very well,' he said. 'Very well. I will remember this. And so will the Pasha. And as for you, Yasmin—!'

Yasmin hastily scuttled ahead of him as he left the yard.

⁂

'Well, that was telling him!' said the villagers appreciatively. There was a little group of them gathered behind the wall. Owen saw them as he came through the gate.

'He deserved it. Why couldn't he speak up for Sabri's boy?'

'He doesn't speak for the village these days. It's all Pasha now.'

'It always was.'

'It's got worse. Ever since the war started, the Pasha's had no time for us. His mind is on other things, and where his mind is, so is Osman's!'

'You'd expect it, wouldn't you, at a time like this? After all, blood is thicker than water.'

'All the same, he could have spoken up for Sabri's boy.'

They saw Owen and invited him to join them for tea. They hadn't forgotten his intervention on behalf of Ibrahim's donkey. As he walked along with them he heard some of them talking behind him.

'That girl's a bit of a handful, isn't she?'

'A girl of spirit!'

'Maybe, but who would want her for a wife?'

'Perhaps Suleiman would. He's a fine young man and not married yet.'

'Me?' said Suleiman, a thin, shy youth. He looked terrified.

'I think she needs someone who is older. Someone with a bit of weight.'

'To keep her down?'

They all laughed.

'He'd have a job!'

'How does she come to know Sabri's woman?' Owen asked the man beside him.

'Fatima was her wet nurse. The girl's mother, you see, is Osman's sister. She used to live here but went in to the city when she got married. Well, after the girl was born, she found she couldn't give her enough milk so she brought her back out here and looked for a woman. She said that a village woman's milk would be better than a city woman's. Sabri's wife had just lost her child—not Salah, it was an earlier one—so she took the girl on. Later, of course, when she had built up a bit of strength, her mother took her back to the city. But the girl has always remembered the one who nursed her. She comes back to see her every time she's out here.'

'You would have thought that might have counted with Osman when it came to Sabri's boy,' said another man. 'But it didn't.'

They came to a house and trooped into the yard. It was big enough to take them all. They squatted round in a circle while cups were fetched and the kettle on the brazier brought to a boil.

The men on the other side of the circle were still talking about Osman Huq.

'I'll bet Osman was surprised when Sabri said the Mamur Zapt would speak for him!'

'He thought it was a lot of old nonsense until Sabri said he was actually going to see him. But when he heard that, I'll bet he started thinking.'

'He should have started thinking before.' The men looked at Owen. 'Do you think you'll be able to bring it off, Effendi? Get this waquf for Salah?'

'Oh, yes, I think so.'

'It would be good if you could.'

'It's funny how it's turned out,' said another man, musing: 'that Sabri should get his way in the end.'

There was a tap on the gate and the donkey-barber slipped into the yard, to everyone's surprise.

'Hello, Anji! What are you doing here?'

'I thought you were over at the Canal?'

'And so I was.'

'There aren't any donkeys here, you know. They're all over where you've just come from.'

'The trouble is, the donkey-barbers are all there too. As I found when I got there.'

'So you've come away? That was a mistake!'

'Not as much of a one as you might think,' said the donkey-barber, grinning. 'I've been working my way back down the road clipping the donkeys before they got there!'

There was a burst of laughter.

'He's a wily bastard, that Anji!'

'But what's all this?' said the donkey-barber, looking round him. 'What is happening in the village? The wise sit here, taking counsel with the Mamur Zapt, while Osman Huq, when I go to see him, sweeps me aside with a face like thunder!'

'I'd go and see him tomorrow if I were you,' said someone. 'He's just had a brush with Sabri's woman.'

'Sabri's woman?'

'You'll be sorry you missed it, Anji. It was worth hearing.'

'If she was telling him a few truths, then I'm sorry indeed.'

'What were you going to see him about, Anji?' asked someone curiously.

'Will you believe it, I was actually trying to do him a favour? Somebody had given me a message for him. Well, he can bloody wait for it now.'

The discussion moved back to the possible waquf. The donkey-barber listened intently. 'If the Mamur Zapt can secure that for the boy,' he said approvingly, 'then that is good. What this country needs is education.'

It was a remark that was widely heard these days and could well have come from Mahmoud or Mohammed Sekhmet. Sabri, too, probably. But to hear it even from a donkey-barber's lips was a little surprising. Donkey-barbers were not usually so solicitous of the nation's well-being. He remarked as much to his neighbour.

'Anji is interested in such things,' the man said.

'From where comes this interest?'

'I do not know. He has always been like that.' The man smiled. 'And much good it has done him! He was thrown out of the madrissa for asking too many questions. Or perhaps knowing too many answers.'

'As a boy was this?'

'No, no. He was a teacher.'

'And then became a donkey-barber? That is strange!'

'He said it suited him and was what he wanted to do.' The man smiled. 'And that it was a job from which no one could dismiss him. He is a card, that man!'

Owen looked up and saw that the donkey-barber was watching him.

'Effendi,' he said, with a mischievous grin, 'since you are in the mood to do good, do you think you could put in a word for me at the Camel Market?'

'Certainly,' said Owen. 'I will tell them that if they seek a man who flies eagerly from where the work is, it is to Anji that they should turn.'

The group roared with laughter.

'In that case,' said the donkey-barber, pretending to be cast down, 'perhaps I shall not ask that the word come directly from the Mamur Zapt's own lips but will make it my own. I shall say to all those I meet with on the road that they must get their donkeys shorn before they arrive at the Canal. By order of the Mamur Zapt.'

Salah was jealously guarding his horse beneath the lebbek trees.

'I have seen he has had water, Effendi,' he said importantly.

'That is good, for I have a long ride back.'

Salah held the horse's head for him.

'Will you come again, Effendi?' he said, almost wistfully.

'No doubt. But perhaps I will see you in the city if you go to the great madrissa there.'

'I would like that.'

He walked along beside Owen as he rode to the end of the village.

'Anji is here,' he said suddenly.

'Yes.'

'He says that soldiers will come to the village shortly and take all the men away.'

'Not all.'

'He says the omda will choose. And he says that when the turn comes, I must go into the desert and hide. For the omda will choose me.'

'You are too young.'

'Nevertheless, he says, the omda will choose me. For he will do what Osman bids him, and Osman does not like me.'

'That is possible.'

'It is because of my father. But Anji says, why should the sins of the father be visited on the child? And he bade me make sure I hid myself.'

'It might be wise to do as he said.'

'Yes.'

As the boy walked along beside him, some of the flies gathered thickly on the horse's flanks flew on to him, dotting his white galabeah and turban with black spots.

'I would not mind fighting,' the boy said. 'But Anji says the men are wanted not to fight but to dig. Anyway, he said, it would be foolish to fight, for it is not Egypt's quarrel, and we would be firing on our brothers.'

He was silent for a moment, and then he said: 'I would not want to dig. Digging is slave's work. That is what my father used to say. He said that all in Egypt are slaves to the land, and it is the Pasha's land, not theirs. He said that that was not for him, nor for me, either. That is why he wanted me to go to the madrissa in the city. "The madrissa costs much, but it buys freedom," he said. "And that is right, for freedom should have a high price."'

'We will see if we can pay that price.'

'I said to my father: "Father, I would prefer to ride with you among the Bedawin." And he said, no, that it had been right for him, because he could not go to the madrissa, and there was no other way out; but it would not be right for me. "To think that freedom lies among the Bedawin," he said, "is an illusion. For they are as bound as we are. They belong to the past. The world has moved on, and nowadays it is the effendi in the great offices who are the free men."'

'I said: "I would not like to work in an office, Father." And he said: "Did I not say that freedom had a price?" He said that these days the Bedawin amounted to nothing, that no one in the desert could ever amount to anything. Even the Senussi, he said, amounted to nothing. They fought bravely against the Italians, he said, and they even managed to hold them; but the Italians were the future and they could not hold out against that. And it would be the same again now, he said. Their tents would cover the land but the British would prevail.'

'It is not necessary for you to go into the great offices,' said Owen. 'The freedom that the madrissa gives is the freedom to choose.'

Salah thought about it.

'I will go to the madrissa, then.'

'I will see to it quickly. It would be well if you were away from the village when the soldiers come.'

Further along the river bank a fire was blazing. They were probably burning the husks, thought Owen. He could see a number of men there throwing things into the flames. It would be hot work on an afternoon like this.

The track turned inland from the river, however, and there were two fields in between him and the pyre when he passed it. Ahead of him he could see some palms and a small, disused white building, an old shrine perhaps.

He was just entering the palms when Yasmin stepped out onto the track in front of him.

He brought his horse to a halt and then, as she went on standing firmly in his way, dismounted.

'I wish to have words with you,' said Yasmin.

She led him under the trees and they sat down on a low wall in front of the shrine.

'Why are you interested in Sabri?' she said abruptly.

'I was there when he was found.'

Yasmin made an impatient gesture.

'And he was coming to see me when he died,' said Owen.

'To report?'

Owen considered.

'Not really,' he said. 'Sabri did not exactly report.'

'He was one of your men, though?'

'Up to a point. If he came across any information that he thought would interest me, he would come to me.'

'And you would pay for it?'

'If I thought it was worthwhile. Or, rather, if my man thought it was worthwhile. I never spoke to Sabri myself.'

'But he was your man?'

'In a manner of speaking.'

'One of your spies!' she spat out.

Owen sighed.

'Why do you sigh?' said Yasmin, after a moment.

Owen did not reply at once. The he said:

'The world thinks that Egypt is full of spies. People think, for instance, that you are a spy.'

'Me?' said Yasmin, astonished.

'And, in a way, you are. Or would be if you could. You would pass information to the Turks, wouldn't you?'

'I certainly would!'

'But you're not really a spy. You're like everyone else in Egypt, you've got all sorts of loyalties.'

'Not everyone,' said Yasmin. 'You, for instance. Your loyalty is to the British.'

'Of course. But not just.'

'Who else are you loyal to?' said Yasmin sceptically.

'Egypt.'

Yasmin flushed.

'You are mocking me!'

'No, I'm not. I live here and I work here and I want what is best for Egypt.'

'You want what is best for Britain!' said Yasmin.

Owen sighed again.

Yasmin was silent for quite some time. The horse found some grass beneath the trees and moved away. On the river bank the fire was still blazing. Above them the doves cooed and gurgled.

'It is true,' said Yasmin suddenly, 'that in Egypt we are pulled in all sorts of directions. Especially a family like mine. And especially at the present time. We are Turkish-Egyptian. My mother's family came here from Turkey with the pashas and has remained true to them ever since. Osman works for the Pasha Ismail and the men of the family have always worked for him or his forebears. My mother, too, would stay true to them. She would like Egypt to return to being part of the Ottoman Empire.

'But I would not. I would like to see the British out of Egypt, yes, but I would not like to see the Turks back in their place. I want Egypt to stand on its own feet, to be Egyptian.

'My father would like that, too, but he would like to go back to the old days of the Khedive. Turkish-Egyptian, but not Turkish. And go back, too, to the old Muslim certainties.

'My brother is like him in that, only somehow it always comes out worse in him. But he is not like me, he follows my mother, staying true to her side of the family. So we are all pulled in different ways.' Yasmin shrugged. 'Like Egypt.'

'That is true. And so we all have to make accommodations. My friend, Mahmoud, for instance, who has views very like your own—'

'Your friend, Mahmoud? Well, yes, I suppose he is your friend. But how *can* he be your friend,' she broke out, 'when you are English?'

'We have been friends for a long time.'

'He may be your friend,' said Yasmin, bitterly, 'but he is not mine. Why is he so severe on me?' she demanded. 'I am on his side!'

'He believes you are still too young for political activity. And, don't forget, he knows the costs.'

'I think he is down on me because I am a woman. I tried to speak with Aisha about this but she just laughed and wouldn't talk about it.'

Yasmin continued to brood.

'Why is he so severe? *You* are not severe.'

The fire on the river bank was beginning to die down. The flames had given way to a thick, grey smoke.

Yasmin looked up with alarm.

'My brother will soon be here. I told him I would walk over to the shrine. He wanted to stay and watch the fire. He likes fires.'

Owen wondered what it was that she had wanted to say to him. Nothing, perhaps. Perhaps she had just wanted to talk to him, intrigued, perhaps, by the fact that he was an Englishman.

He got up and went to find his horse.

Suddenly Yasmin came running after him.

'I need to know about Sabri,' she said urgently. 'I need to.'

Owen saw a figure coming quickly across the fields towards them. He climbed back up on to his horse.

'What do you want to know?' he said.

'Why did Sabri have to die?' she whispered. 'Why?'

As Owen was riding away, he caught sight of her brother's angry face.

Chapter Thirteen

Owen felt uneasy about Yasmin and, a couple of days later, as he was crossing the Ataba el Khadra, he thought he would drop in at the fire station to have a word with Mohammed Sekhmet.

A training drill was going on in the yard. One of the small two-horsed engines had been brought out and its crew were busily running out a hose. One took the nozzle and dashed over to a practice wall, another fastened the other end of the hose to a hydrant, and another pushed out the escape ladder. Another man was standing by with a watch.

'One minute seven seconds,' he said.

The firemen were all in their thick blue uniforms and wearing glittering brass helmets pointed on top. In the heat it must have been sweltering but they all grinned cheerfully at Owen.

The crew lowered the ladder and began to run the hose back to the cart. One of the men jumped up on to the cart to see to the coiling. The man with the watch stood by keeping a careful eye.

'It's important, Effendi,' he explained to Owen. 'If they're not coiled right, they won't run out right. And, besides, it's bad for the hoses.'

Along one side of the yard was a row of stables. Owen could see the noses of the horses pointing out above the half-doors. The fire engines themselves were drawn up in the middle of the yard, three two-horse ones and a larger four-horse one. The larger one was now being brought out in place of the two-horse one, which was being pulled aside.

The crew of the larger engine stood looking expectantly at the man with the watch.

'Now!' he said, and immediately they set to work, running out the hose and a huge eighty foot ladder. One of the firemen mounted the ladder with a nozzle and a moment later was directing a fierce 1¼-inch jet against the target, with the aid of a steamer from the motor tower.

'Two minutes nine seconds,' said the man with the watch.

'Pretty good,' said Owen.

'We need to be,' said the man with the watch.

The crew were in the middle of storing the hose away when a man dashed out into the yard and banged a gong.

'Damn!' said the man with the watch. He touched Owen on the arm. 'However, Effendi,' he said, 'watch this!'

Before the echoes of the gong had died away, a man ran round opening the half-doors of the stables. The horses came out of their own accord.

'There!' said the man with the watch proudly.

By now firemen were leading the horses to two of the carts. A moment later they were racing out of the great gates of the fire station clanging their bells.

'I am most impressed,' Owen said to Mohammed Sekhmet a little later when he went into his office.

'Thank you, Effendi,' said Mohammed Sekhmet gravely.

'It is good to see such zeal and such efficiency. They are things one does not always see in Egypt.'

'And in England?' asked Mohammed Sekhmet.

'Not in England, either.'

Mohammed Sekhmet seemed unusually subdued this morning. After greeting Owen he sat down again behind his desk as looked at his hands.

'Well, Effendi,' he said, 'what can I do for you?'

'I wanted to have a word with you about Yasmin.'

'You have seen her, I gather,' said Mohammed Sekhmet, not looking up from his hands.

'Yes, I was out at the village a couple of days ago.'

'To see Yasmin?'

'No, no. On other business. It was just that she was at one of the houses I visited.'

'But then you spoke with her again.'

'By accident, yes.'

'Alone.'

'I met her on the road as I was riding back to Cairo.'

'Yes. Osman has told me. And my son.'

'Oh, yes.'

'Effendi, I think you should not speak to Yasmin again. I believe you mean well, but it unsettles her and disturbs my family.'

'Certainly, if that is what you wish.'

'It is what I wish.' He looked up from his hands. 'What was it you wanted to say to me, Effendi?'

What Owen had wanted to say was that he did not think the village, or Osman's household, the right place for Yasmin. It was too crippling for a girl of her intelligence and Osman's regime too harsh and lacking in understanding.

But now he felt he could not say that. What business was it of his? It was evidently a family matter and however much you might feel that the family was wrong, you could not interfere. And this was especially so with women in an Egyptian family.

Yet he felt he had to say something.

'You should not think,' he said quietly, 'that because your original intentions for Yasmin have not turned out the way you expected, they were necessarily wrong.'

'They were wrong,' said Mohammed Sekhmet flintily, 'and God has rebuked me.' He stood up to show Owen out. 'Yasmin will marry a man from the village, a man who will keep her within her proper horizons. It is not as I would have wished, I had hoped for better things for her. But what is more important than worldly achievement is that she should do right in the eye of God. She must learn to find her fulfillment in the performance of her wifely duties.'

When Owen came out into the sunlight of the yard, the heat hit him like a fist. He stopped for a moment, quite dazed. Over on the other side of the courtyard some firemen were gathered round a bucket which seemed to have some sort of hand-pump in it. Nearby was a small heap of rubbish, wooden boxes, packaging. The man with the watch was there again.

'Right,' he said. 'Let's start. Who's going to light it?'

There was a sudden chorus.

'Fahmy, Fahmy! Fahmy's the one.'

A man came forward sheepishly.

'Right, then, Fahmy. Get on with it!'

A man stooped and put a match to the pile of rubbish.

'One!' said the watch keeper.

Someone seized the pump and began to work it. Another took its small hose and directed a jet on to the rubbish.

'Two, three,' counted the watch keeper.

Another bucket was brought and the man making the pump transferred it dexterously.

'Eight, nine. Stop! Well, that wasn't bad,' said the man with the watch. He turned and saw Owen. 'Just a little one this time, Effendi,' he said with a grin. 'We use this sometimes when we can't get the hose there.'

The men around the pump looked up. One of them, the man who had lit the fire, was Yasmin's brother. And again the angry look came over his face when he saw Owen.

Nikos had asked for a meeting of himself, Georgiades, Owen, and the financial expert from Customs. He said that in the course of the financial negotiation over the cotton something had come up on which they needed Owen's guidance.

They gathered in Owen's office. Georgiades was looking even greyer in the face. When Owen asked him how his wife's deal was progressing, he just shook his head despairingly.

Nikos said that Iskander, the middle man who was acting for
the Pasha Ismail, had just introduced a new demand. The Pasha
wanted payment not in money but in rifles, which were to go
to an agent of his in Tripoli. Iskander said that was no problem,
that he could arrange for the purchase and dispatch of the arms.
It just meant that when Georgiades received the money from
the European buyer, he would allow Iskander to draw on it for
the necessary purchasing. Georgiades would, of course, retain a
balance until the deal was concluded.

'This kind of three-way transaction is quite normal,' said the
financial expert from Customs, 'and it doesn't affect the legal
issue, which is the illicit export of cotton. But we thought that,
given the nature of the consignment, and where the arms are
going, we ought to check it with you.'

'Rifles?' said Owen. 'Tripoli?'

'The war is over now,' the Customs official pointed out.

The war with Italy had ended not long before.

'So why do they want the arms?'

'I imagine the ultimate buyer will be the Senussi,' said the
Customs man. 'They probably need to replenish their stocks.'

'As a general principle, we are reluctant to see the tribes of
the interior more heavily armed,' said Owen.

'That's what we thought. I think what it comes down to is
at what point do we wish to intervene, bring the whole thing
to a halt.'

'When we've got enough to nail Ismail. Have we got to that
point, do you think?'

'Probably.'

'I was really hoping to see the cotton physically moving. That
way there's less scope for argument.'

'Well, we've probably got to that state now,' said Nikos.
'Georgiades could ask for it.'

'We've got people down in Ossawa watching the crop,' said
the Customs official.

'Ossawa?'

'The Pasha's estate. Ismail has got estates all over the place, but that's the one the sample came from. According to old Zaghlul.'

Ossawa. He had come across the name recently. Ah, yes: that was where the donkey-barber had brought the message for Osman Huq from. From one of the Pasha Ismail's estates to another, probably.

Something was niggling at the back of his mind.

'I thought old Zaghlul said the estate was on the river?'

'It is on the river. Most Pashas' estates are. That's where the fertile land is.'

'But—'

The donkey-barber had given the impression that he had been working the Canal road. But that road lay across the desert. He had made a detour, obviously. No reason why he shouldn't. But—

And now another thought began to niggle: something else that the man from Customs had said.

∞

'I've been to the hospital,' said Zeinab.

'Oh, yes?'

'Labiba took me. It was terrible there. There are so many wounded coming in from Gallipoli that it's frightfully over-crowded. The staff are completely swamped.'

'It was pretty full when I was there.'

'It's worse now. There are people lying on the floor between the beds and on mattresses down the middle. They're going to have to open an annexe. That's why Labiba was there.'

'She's going to do it?'

Zeinab nodded.

'That's what Cairns-Grant wants. In fact, he's insisting on it. I've never seen him so angry. Of course, he's very tired. He looks exhausted. But he was furious. Paul had been there all day trying to calm him down.'

'Well, he's being left to carry the whole damned thing. And with the numbers—'

'It's not that. Or not just that. There are some Egyptians there. They want to move them out.'

'They?'

'Mrs Cunningham says that her teams could manage extra wards. But the Egyptians don't like being nursed by women. They think it's improper for women to do that sort of thing. If they can be moved out, Australians could be put in that ward, or those wards, there are three of them now, apparently, and Mrs Cunningham's teams could manage the lot, without any extra staffing.'

'What about the ordinary nursing staff?'

'They're run off their feet as it is.'

'Can't they get in some more?'

'That's just what they're doing. Only they have to train them first.'

'What about the German nuns?'

'They're assisting the specialist nurses with the emergency cases. Cairns-Grant says that's too important to leave to a lot of well-meaning…biddies, I think he said, I didn't quite catch the word!'

Owen disappeared into the kitchen to fetch Zeinab a cold drink. When he came back, he said:

'So they're going to do it? Move the Egyptians out, I mean?'

'It appears so. Paul insists it's not out. It's merely to another part of the hospital. That's what the annexe would be, he says. Just another part of the hospital.'

'But for Egyptians only?'

'Because of the nursing problem. Only because of that. They say.'

'It's foolish as well as nasty. How do they think Egyptian politicians are going to react?'

'Paul swears that the facilities will be at least as good. If they're not, he says he will offer himself up to Labiba for vivisection.'

'How does Labiba come into it?'

'Cairns-Grant says that if the annexe is genuinely going to be part of the hospital, then that means he has the say over who runs it. And he says Labiba.'

'What about the other doctors?'

'He says they will support him to a man. And they are, of course, all men.'

'I know, but…. Professional solidarity and all that.'

'I talked to one of them. He said he'd trained in the medical faculty when Labiba's husband was Dean and that he'd known her for years. He had great respect for her, they all had. And then he said: "Look, Zeinab, at the moment I'm working eighteen hours a day, and that's the way it should be. But I want to spend it using my medical expertise. I don't want to be running round chasing people and bits of paper. I know Labiba is a terrific administrator and, as far as I'm concerned, the sooner she gets started, the better."'

'The nurses will all be men. Even the new ones. Might not that cause difficulty?'

'I said that to Mahfouz. He said that people tended to do what Labiba told them.'

Owen sipped his drink. Then a thought occurred to him.

'What were you doing there?'

'I told you. Labiba took me.'

'Why did Labiba take you?'

'She wanted me to see for myself. She said that when people saw for themselves, it was very hard for them not to do something.'

'To do something? Exactly what—?'

'This annexe will be up and running within a month. Labiba says that when it is, she will need help.'

'And you—?'

'Yes.' Zeinab drained her glass. 'And meanwhile,' she said firmly, 'I am going to work in the general wards to learn what it's all about.'

One of the orderlies came to him from the orderly office at the front of the building.

'Effendi, there's a man been hanging around.'

'Oh, yes.'

There were always people hanging around in Egypt; especially around the Bab-el-Khalk.

'We didn't like the look of him so we sent Selim to talk to him.'

'Yes?'

'Effendi, I think you ought to talk to Selim.'

Owen went downstairs and out through the main door. Selim was standing at the bottom of the steps.

'Hello, Selim. What's the problem?'

'There's no problem, Effendi—Now. I sent the daft bastard away.'

'Was he being a nuisance?'

'Not really, Effendi. He was just hanging around. But he was magnoum, crazy—and they didn't like the look of him.'

'He went off without making any trouble?'

'He was a bit truculent. He asked what the hell I was doing, ordering him around. I said I was a policeman and that's what policemen did. He said I was in the pay of the British. And I said it was true that they paid me and I wouldn't work for them unless they did.'

'What did he say to that?'

'He said that the British were infidels and that the new lot who had come—I think he meant the Australians, Effendi—were even worse. They didn't follow God's holy commandments. I said, well, of course, they wouldn't, coming from far away and not knowing them. He said they drank and they swore and they went with women. I said that amazed me.

'That was when he become truculent, Effendi. He said I was a flouter and a scoffer and a mocker of the Holy Word and that God's wrath would be visited on me as surely as it would on the infidels. So I told him to piss off.'

'Well, you seem to have dealt with that very effectively, Selim. If he causes any more trouble, perhaps you'd let me know?'

Selim walked back with him up the steps.

'I think it's the heat, Effendi. It sort of brings them out. Crazy people like this, I mean.'

They stopped at the top of the steps.

'The fact is, Effendi, I think I know this person. He works at the fire station.'

'At the fire station?'

'Yes. He's one of the firemen. I thought I'd go round there, Effendi, when I come off duty, and have a word with Hamid. He's a friend of mine. I thought I'd tell him to keep an eye on this bloke, and maybe turn the hose on him from time to time to cool him down.'

❦

'I've received another invitation,' said Zeinab.

'Samira again?'

'Not this time. It's from Delila. But it will be the same people, and with the same aim.'

'Don't go.'

'I won't.' Zeinab put the letter away.

The next day, however, the invitation was renewed.

'She says it won't be like the other party. There will be just a few friends. It will be a family occasion and the purpose is to welcome a cousin who has just returned to the city.'

'If it were just that...'

'She swears it is.'

'I'll bet Faruq will be there, though.'

'Very probably. I won't go.'

'It seems a pity to miss out, though, if it is really is a family do. Who's the cousin?'

Zeinab consulted the letter.

'Ismail.'

Owen sat up.

'Ismail? Is he a Pasha?'

'Yes.'

'Which Ismail? He doesn't, by any chance, have an estate at Ossawa?'

'I think that's the one, yes. The trouble with a large family is that it's hard to keep track of them.'

'Does he know Faruq?'

'I don't know.'

'It would be interesting to find out.'

'Are you trying to use me, too?' demanded Zeinab.

'Okay, forget about it. Don't go.'

There was a little silence.

'Why do you want to know?' said Zeinab.

'It doesn't matter.'

'Work?'

'It could be.'

'Is it political?'

'Very.'

Zeinab considered.

'I think you ought to tell me.'

'Look, I don't want you to go. Not if you're going to be mucked about by Faruq.'

'Tell me.'

'I'm wondering—and it is just wondering—about possible ways in which information might get from the Sultan's Office to friends of the Turks.'

'Secret information?'

'Yes.'

'About the war? Military information?'

'Yes.'

They were inside. Zeinab was lying on the divan, Owen was sprawled on two of the big leather cushions on the floor.

Zeinab swung her feet down and went out on to the balcony. She stood leaning against the rail, looking down at the square below, with a solitary arabeah parked beneath the trees and a few people talking by the kiosk which sold newspapers, and then outward and across to where it was just possible to make out the heads of the palms beside the river bank and, further still, two feluccas bending across the water.

Owen followed her out and stood beside her.

'I'm not doing anything for the British,' said Zeinab.

'No.'

'Don't forget, I'm part Turkish.'

'Turkish-Egyptian.'

'More Egyptian than Turkish.'

'I know.'

'Where does Egypt come in all this?'

Owen thought.

'I don't know,' he confessed.

'At least you're honest,' said Zeinab.

'I don't even know what "Egypt" is in this connection. It's obviously the Egypt of the British. But apart from that? Is it the Egypt of the Pashas? Or is it the Egypt of the fellahin? Or is it the Egypt of the Nationalists? I just don't know.'

'Join the rest of us,' said Zeinab.

Owen had a meeting of the Intelligence Committee the next morning. It was a strange meeting. Everyone's minds seemed somewhere else. Which they were. All the Intelligence reports showed that a Turkish attack was imminent. The main purpose of the meeting seemed to be to show that all available resources were being hurried up to the Canal. Owen indicated his reservations.

'I know, I know,' said Cavendish. 'The Senussi. But they're miles away in the West, if they're there at all and not happily riding round the Sahara, and meanwhile the Turks are just next door poised to come across the Canal at any moment.'

No one else said anything. They were all anxious to get away. Not unreasonably, thought Owen. Committees seemed a bit irrelevant just at the moment.

They finished early.

He stopped Paul for a word after the meeting.

'Yes, yes, I know,' said Paul. 'The annexe. Well, look, they've got to have an annexe. The hospital is bursting at the seams. And what happens when the wounded start coming in after engagement opens on the Canal?'

'It's the segregation I don't like. Egyptians and the rest.'

'It won't last. There'll be so many wounded coming in that they'll have to use the annexe for all-comers. And the great thing is, it'll be under Labiba. Not that bloody woman Cunningham.'

'Yes, well, I do see that's an advantage. I'm getting really fed up with the way she carries on.'

'Yes, well, so am I. Don't forget I spent all Tuesday trying to calm Cairns-Grant down, and half the problem was getting her to shut up.'

'You know, I'm going to have to have a go at her.'

'Gareth, please, please! Can you stay out of this? Could you just leave this to me? This is war time and we can't afford to have non-combatants like me. And so I have decided to take a hand. And the first thing I propose to do is open a private front against Mrs Cunningham. The battle plan is already worked out, so I don't want you butting in. First, I intend to build up someone else, then I shall find an issue which divides the enemy and on which Mrs C feels obliged to make a stand. Then I shall bring it to a head and force her out.

'This is a matter of military tactics, Gareth, and I am practising so that I can take over in place of the Commander-in-Chief should the need arise. After Mrs Cunningham, I imagine the Turks will be easy.'

~

Zeinab went to her party. The mood, she said, was jubilant. The Turkish attack was expected at any moment and everyone was confident that when it came it would be successful. People talked excitedly about the changes that would be made: the changes at Court, that was, and in the Ministries, which were the only changes that interested them. Faruq was already making dispositions.

He was there, of course. However, so caught up in the general excitement was he, and with the consequences of Turkish success, that he paid little attention to Zeinab; remarking only, with heavy significance, on one occasion that when the time came she would 'soon see.'

It was taken for granted that Zeinab shared the pro-Turkish sentiment of the group and, for once, Zeinab didn't fall into argument. It was astonishing, she observed afterward to Owen, how rapidly, after so many years, the Pashas were rediscovering their Turkish roots. What she was conscious of in herself was the great distance that had grown up between herself and the circles into which she had been born. The discovery that she had been experiencing lately had been that of Egypt outside those circles, a bigger, less privileged, more confused but certainly more exciting Egypt than the one she had known.

She left as soon as she could and was amused, and touched, to find Owen waiting just outside the door. 'In case of accidents,' he said.

She had spoken to the Pasha Ismail, but only briefly. He had spent most of the evening in conversation with Faruq.

The Turkish attack came the next day. Intelligence reports had given the British a pretty good idea of where the main strike would be and they had been able to assemble enough forces to hold it. Some Turkish units did succeed in crossing the Canal but were forced back with the aid of the fire from two French cruisers and a sandstorm. The fighting continued for several days but the Turks were unable to make the break they had hoped for.

They had hoped that the civilian population would rise against the British, but they did not. Owen had thought they might and McPhee had had his policemen at the ready; for all the good that was likely to do. They did not need to be called on, however. The country remained quiet. The Egyptians, wisely, had decided to wait and see who emerged as the winner before taking sides.

The Turkish attacks petered out and there was a lull in hostilities. And it was just at this moment that the Senussi attacked. They swept into the country from the west and occupied a few frontier towns.

And now Owen knew the message that Sabri had been trying to get to him.

Chapter Fourteen

The Intelligence Committee held an emergency meeting.

'Got any more nasty surprises for us, Owen?' said one of the Army officers, as they trooped into the committee room.

'It wasn't a surprise to Owen,' Cavendish said quietly. 'It was to us and it ought not to have been. We had been told. We'll have to do some thinking about that.'

The Army representatives had the grace to admit that was so.

They were feeling pleased with themselves. The battle had gone their way and the Turks had been held.

'Next time it will be our turn,' they promised.

'That won't be for some time yet,' said Lawrence. 'And meanwhile? What are we going to do about the Senussi?'

'They won't come far into Egypt,' said Owen. 'They're raiders, not occupiers.'

'We'll have to send somebody to chase them out,' said one of the officers.

The senior officer looked unhappy.

'It's too early to detach people yet,' he said. 'The Turks may come again.'

'In any case we've got everyone up on the Canal,' said Paul. 'Just what Gareth was worried about.'

'We could transfer the Camel Corps,' said Owen. 'They're less use at the Canal, where it's a static war. One for the infantry. But over in the West it will be camels against camels.'

'And they'd get over there a bit more quickly,' said Paul.

'Can we rely on them, though?' asked one of the officers. 'I know the officers would be British, but—'

'You can rely on them,' said Owen. 'There might be a question as to how far the Egyptians see the Turks as their enemy. But there's no question at all as to how they see the Senussi. They've been fighting the Senussi for centuries.'

⟡

The next week or two was rather a strange period. On the Canal fighting continued for some time but in a desultory way. There were occasional sorties which would sometimes develop into quite heavy engagements but the British grew increasingly confident of their ability to contain them. In the West, the Camel Corps, transferred with great speed, was very soon making an impact. For a time there was sharp skirmishing but then the Senussi were found to withdraw behind their own borders. They made occasional raids but for the most part were content to circle and threaten.

In between, however, things were quiet.

Except in the hospitals. While casualties weren't heavy, either at the Canal or against the Senussi, certainly compared with the losses at Gallipoli, the wounded were soon coming in such numbers as to exhaust the little spare capacity that existed in the Cairo and Alexandria hospitals. The need for the annexe became imperative. It wouldn't become operable for at least another fortnight, however, and meanwhile the wounded were already arriving.

Zeinab was drawn into nursing. She threw herself into it with all her abundant energy and Owen didn't see her from six in the morning until midnight, when she came home so exhausted that she collapsed straight into bed. She had no time to speak to him and he had no idea how she was getting on, so one day he went along to the hospital to see.

The conditions in the hospital were much worse than when he had been there before. Indeed, they were appalling. Wounded men now covered the floor everywhere. They lay along the corridors, they had spread out even on to the verandahs and down the steps. He had to step over them on his way to Cairns-Grant's office.

The Australians were still gambling and the startled lizards dropping their tails. A sizeable proportion of them, however, had now dropped them and the majority of the lizards skirting over the walls were strangely stumpy.

Zeinab came into the ward and was at once greeted with a warm chorus.

'Over here, sweetheart!'

'Oh, you're a beaut!'

'This way, Sheila! Never mind him.'

Zeinab smiled, waved a hand to Owen, reached under a bed and hurried out carrying a bed-pan.

'Hey! She waved to him! What's this guy got that I haven't got?'

'Well, two legs, both arms, a nose in the right place…and that's before we get down to essentials!'

In the office Cairns-Grant was talking to Labiba Latifa.

'I know, lassie, but you're needed over there. It'll be ready in ten days and we need someone to make sure they're putting things in the right places.'

'I'll go over there this afternoon.'

'And stay there, love. You're more use over there.'

'I'll show them where the stuff's got to go and then come back. The new equipment won't start coming till next week.'

'Aye, but we're transferring some of the equipment from here.'

'Alec, there's a thing about that. Mrs Cunningham is saying—'

'I know what Mrs Cunningham is saying.'

'Yes, but she's insisting—'

'Aye, and young Trevelyan is insisting, too. And, what's more, he's got the Commissioner behind him!'

'She says she will resign!'

'I think,' said Owen, 'that that may be the idea.'

⁕

He had spoken with the Ministry and they had found a waquf that Salah could benefit from. His mother brought him in and took him to the school. They liked him and after a few tests his entry was agreed upon. Afterwards, Salah came round to thank Owen.

'I am not sure, though, Effendi, that this is what I want. I know my father would have wished it and so I will do it. But I would have preferred a man's job.'

'That time will come. Meanwhile, there is something you can do for me which is very much a man's job.'

'Tell me, Effendi.'

'It touches your father's death.'

'Then I shall not fail you, Effendi.'

'Your father went to see Osman to speak with him. It was, in fact, about yourself. Now, what I want to know is: did a man go afterwards from Osman, or from the village, to the Camel Market? Take care how you find out. For if it is not done secretly, those who encompassed your father's death might connive at yours.'

'I understand, Effendi.'

'Do this,' said Owen, 'and afterwards the men of the village will know that it was your hand that was on the avenging dagger.'

∞

'Hello, Selim. How are you today? Are there any magnum fellows hanging around, or have you chased them all away?'

'None today, Effendi. I think it is because the weather is cooler.' The big policeman fell in beside him.

'I spoke to Hamid the other day, Effendi. You know, my friend at the fire station. It was about that magnum fellow. It was as I thought, Effendi. He did come from the fire station. In fact, he's one of the firemen. They know all about him. They say he is a real pain in the ass. He's always on to them, chiding them for their profanity. Well, I mean, Effendi, if a man can't use a few choice words occasionally, especially when he's a firemen, where the hell are you? It's worse than being a policeman. Well, perhaps not worse, but nearly as bad as.

'He's always popping into the mosque, too. Well, that's all right, so we should. But you've got to choose the right time. That's what I tell my wives. Not when I want my bloody supper,

I say. Anyway, he goes in every time he gets back from a fire, to give thanks, I suppose. Well, that's all right you may think, but that, of course, is just when they're busy. The hose pipes have to be hung up and dried and that sort of thing. And he's always in the mosque!

'Well, it gets them down, understandably. They'd like to get rid of him but they can't. He's the son of the boss, you see. "You're got to make allowances," he says. You know, for the poor bastard being magnoum. "He can do his job all right." Well, so he can. It's just that he's a real pain to have around the place.

'They feel they can't do anything. You know, sometimes when there's nothing on, and there's often quite a lot not going on in a fire station, except just lately, of course, they like to have a quiet game of something. "You can't do that!" he says. "It's forbidden!" Well, I'm as devout as the next man but you've got to draw the line somewhere!

'"So," Hamid says, "can you lock this poor bugger up? Just to get him out of the way for a bit? So that we can get on with our game?" And, Effendi, do you know, I've been wondering: could I get him for hanging around, do you think? He does a lot of hanging around, apparently.'

'It depends a bit on where he hangs.'

'I'll certainly get him if he hangs about here.'

'It's not exactly against the law, Selim. Chivvy him off, though, by all means, if he's a nuisance.'

As he continued on up the stairs, a thought struck him. He turned and came down again.

'Selim, that magnoum fellow: you say he does a lot of hanging around. Where?'

'I don't know, Effendi. It's just what the firemen say.'

'Selim, there's a thing I'd like you to do for me. I want you to check—'

⁂

'I think I can say I've played my part,' said Curtis, with modest pride. 'People tend to forget our side of things but without us there couldn't be any fighting. You can fire the bullets only if they're there. Well, they were there, and I'm proud of it. Not just me, of course, but everyone in Supplies. We're part of a great team. That's what I always say, a great team.

'Mind you, we've had our difficulties at times. I'll give you an example. When the Camel Corps was switched from one front to the other to tackle the Senussi. You might think it was just a question of riding across. Well, it was that, of course, but it was also much more. No good arriving there if the bullets hadn't, was it? And not just bullets: food, water, medical supplies—medical supplies are a bit on my mind just at the moment—and fodder.

'You wouln't think of that, would you? Fodder. Fodder for the camels. Indispensable. An army marches on its stomach, they say, and so do camels. Of course, they can go for a long time without food, everyone knows that. But they've got to eat some time. Well, that's my job, to see there are proper supplies for them to eat.

'And, you see, there was a bit of a problem here. We had set up arrangements, of course, but they were all for supplies to the Canal. That's what the contracts were made out for. Well, now, suddenly, they had to be switched. I don't mind telling you it was a nightmare.

'Fortunately, one of our suppliers grasped the situation at once. She—'

'She?'

'Yes. I know it's surprising, out here in Egypt especially. But one of our suppliers is a lady. And a very resourceful one, too. I must admit I had my reservations when she first approached me. But she impressed me, I have to say she impressed me. The discount she was offering—well, it was irresistible. So, against the advice of some of my colleagues, I must say, I went for her. And I haven't regretted it.

'When I told her about the need to switch supplies, she was on to it in a flash. She got in touch with her suppliers immediately and the next moment the loads were streaming the other way.

'Not easy, I can tell you. At such short notice. Besides, she had to use donkeys. There weren't any camels left, you see. The country's been stripped bare of them. My doing, of course. They were needed at the front. I felt I had to apologise. "Don't worry," she said, "I'll see that the fodder gets through."

'And she did. Of course, we had to pay a bit extra for it, but that was only reasonable. There were other obstacles she had to surmount and she didn't charge for those. She told me some of them. When her first caravan got to the other side, that was only the beginning of it. Where the hell was the Camel Corps? I mean, the desert's a big place.

'Well, as luck would have it, her people ran into someone who could help them. A donkey-barber, coming back from further west, Timbuktoo, perhaps, where he had been, to clip donkeys, I suppose. As it happened, he'd seen the Camel Corps riding out and knew roughly where their detachments had gone. So he was able to point the caravan in the right direction. Very helpful in other ways, too. He stopped with them until they deposited their loads and then came back with them. Clipping their donkeys on the way.'

Georgiades was in a state of collapse. His cheeks hung down in great grey pouches, his eyes shifted wearily, sweat ran in streams down his face.

'Yes,' he said, 'it's got worse. She's upped the ante. They wanted her to switch supplies, you see—the Camel Corps has moved over to the west, God know where, off the end of the world probably. And the contract was specifically with them, you see. I said: "This is your chance, Rosa. No one will blame you. The contract says, supply to the Canal. If they don't want it there, that's fine. Do a deal. Terminate the contract—they'll be glad to. Seize the chance. Take whatever money you've got and run."

'But she hasn't done that. In fact, she's done just the opposite. Would you believe it, she's increased the quantities. More fodder, tons more. The others couldn't get their act changed in time and she stepped in.

"'Rosa,' I said, "please! Think of our child. Think of our house!"

"'We haven't got a house,' she said. "All we've got is an apartment. But now I've increased the contract, I'll be able to get a house." She's probably thinking of the Abdin Palace.

"'The risk, Rosa, the risk!' I said. "Think of the risk!"

"'I *am* thinking of the risk,' she said. "I've put the price up.'"

'Has she actually lost any money yet?' asked Owen.

'No. In fact, she's made some. She insisted on part-payment in advance for this latest lot. So she's actually got quite a bit in hand. But it will go nowhere,' concluded Georgiades gloomily, 'when all this collapses about her ears.'

'Well, I don't know what we can do about it.'

'We can't do anything about it,' said Georgiades, sunk in despair. 'We just have to wait for it to happen.'

He looked round the foyer of the hotel, at all the crowded tables, each with its group of besuited men deep in conversation, heads bent forward confidingly.

'You know,' he said, 'I'll almost be glad when it does. The sooner I can get away from anything to do with business, the better. What I want to do is get back on the streets. *Please* put me back on the streets! I want to feel the heat between my shoulders again, I want to smell the peanuts roasting round the Ezbehiyah, the garlic and stale fat and urine of the back streets, I want to see the flies sticking to the candy poles on the stalls, I want to taste the sand and grit in my mouth again. I want to be back.'

'You can be back,' said Owen. 'They're beginning to move the cotton. It's left the estate and has got to the docks. The Customs men will see it go on board and then we will have him.'

'All over?'

'All over, and hardly worth the effort. All they'll do is fine him. On this. However—'

'There's one thing more, though, that I want you to do. When you're saying your farewells to Iskander. Shake him warmly by the hand and thank him and say what a pleasure it's been working with him. Say that unfortunately he won't see you

for a while because you've got to give all your time to something
else. Something big, something so big that it'll make all this—'
he waves his hand at the businessmen in the foyer— 'look like
peanuts. Tell him that there could be something in it for him
if things work out as you hope, and that in a week or two he
can expect a call.

'And, meanwhile, there's a small thing he could do for you.
You'd appreciate it if he could pass on a message for you. To a
gentleman he knows at Ossawa.'

Lawrence was sitting alone in the bar. He looked up at Owen
as he came in but without enthusiasm.

'Hello,' he said.

He didn't offer to buy him a drink. This was less lack of
sociability, Owen thought, than self-sufficiency. Lawrence always
gave the impression of being sufficient to himself. He had few
friends—Paul was the person who came closest—and made few
efforts to acquire any.

Owen didn't buy him a drink, either.

'Things quiet at the office?' he said.

'They'll stay quiet now. The Turks have tried it on and failed.
Now they'll sit back. We'll sit back, too, because no one on our
side has thought what to do next. Sometimes you despair.'

'What would you do next?' asked Owen.

Lawrence looked at him.

'Ah,' he said. He was silent for a moment. Then he said:

'You were right about the Senussi. Not that it'll make much
difference in the end. They'll make a nuisance of themselves over
in the West but they won't come deep into Egypt. They're desert
people. Egypt is a hell of a place for desert people.'

'There's a lot of desert in Egypt,' objected Owen. 'It's mostly
one narrow fertile strip down the Nile.'

'Yes, but it's that fertile strip that makes the difference. In the
desert there's no fertile strip, and people have to live with that.
It makes them different mentally.'

'Bleak,' said Owen.

'You could say that. I don't know that I would,' he shrugged. 'But it's among the desert men that the next bit of the war out here is going to be fought. There'll be a standstill on the Canal. The action will have to take place somewhere else.'

'That's what you would do next?'

'If I had any say in it.' He finished his glass and put it down. 'Actually,' he said, 'I was thinking of going over there and taking a look.'

Good luck, thought Owen. The Empty Quarter, or wherever Lawrence thought he was going, could stay empty as far as he was concerned. Like Georgiades, Owen was a man of the city.

'When are you going?'

'A week or so.'

'I wonder if you could do something for me before you go. Your people on the other side. At the Turkish headquarters.'

'Yes?'

'I'd just like to know if a certain message comes through.'

'What's the message?'

'That the next phase of the battle is likely to be a British invasion across the Red Sea.'

'Don't be daft!'

'By boat. After all, that is something we have got.'

'No one in their right senses has ever contemplated such a thing! Nor would they.'

'I know,' said Owen.

One of the orderlies came along and said that a woman wished to see him. A few moments later she was shown in. She wore the usual dark heavy veil which concealed her head as well as her face, and the usual dark shapeless gown. Owen was surprised to see a woman unaccompanied but took her for a widow and greeted her as such. There was a giggle from behind the veil.

'It's me,' said Yasmin.

'What are you doing here? On your own?'

'I didn't want anyone to know, so I told my uncle that I wanted to collect some things from home. I shall collect them, only I wanted to call in here first.'

'Why?'

'I wanted to see you.'

'Yes?'

'That's it,' said Yasmin. 'I wanted to see you.'

'But—?'

'Do you mind?'

'Well, no. I'm just a bit surprised that's all.'

'I thought you'd like to see me.'

'Well—'

What was she up to? Surely she wasn't flirting with him?

'I like seeing *you*. You're the only one who really talks to me.'

'Well, that's nice, but—'

'I'd like to talk to you more often.'

'I would like to talk to you, too, but—'

'Would you?' said Yasmin. 'Really?'

'Yes, really.'

'You're not just saying that?'

'No. However,' said Owen firmly, 'I think we have to face the probability that we won't be able to.'

Yasmin seemed to acquiesce, although he couldn't really tell, with her so inaccessible behind the heavy veil. She sat silent for a moment. Then she said suddenly:

'Are you married?'

'Married? Yes.'

'To the Lady Zeinab?'

'Yes.'

'They told me you were. She is the daughter of Nuri Pasha, isn't she? I'm against the Pashas. I'm against all privilege.'

'I don't think Zeinab feels very privileged just at the moment. She's working at the hospital.'

'Nursing?'

'Administration, more.'

'I wish I could work,' said Yasmin. 'Work properly, I mean. At something real, something important. Something that would make a difference.'

'You should continue with your studies.'

'Perhaps. However, they're not going to let me. I am going to get married.'

'You are?'

'To a sixty-year-old farmer!' said Yasmin bitterly. 'Osman has already arranged it. And after that there will be no more talk, no more books, no more learning. There will be work, all right, though. In the fields and in the kitchen. For ever and ever and ever.'

'Yasmin, I do not think such a life would be right for you.'

'Nor do I. But what can I do about it? It's all gone wrong, wrong!'

'I'll speak to your father again.'

'He won't listen to you. You're on the wrong side. There are so many wrong sides in Egypt and you're on practically all of them.'

She was silent again.

'I'm glad you've told me all this,' said Owen. 'But it wasn't what you came to see me about, was it?'

Chapter Fifteen

'Sabri was like an uncle to me,' said Yasmin, 'but Sabri's wife was like a mother. I do not remember him from the time I first went to the house. I was too small. I remember him only from the times I used to visit there when I occasionally came back to the village. And then he was like an uncle. He spoke to me courteously and with respect; but we were not close.

'With Fatima it was different. I had taken her milk and looked to her as to a mother. It was as my mother that I always went to see her whenever I returned to the village.

'But as I grew older I became more aware of Sabri. At first he was just a man across the room in the darkness and I paid him no attention. But gradually I began to listen to him. I could not help it because he was always talking. And Fatima talked with him. This surprised me because no one talked in my own house, nor in Osman's house, nor in any of the other houses I knew. I daresay the men talked when they were with other men, but that was always outside the house. What surprised me was that Sabri and Fatima talked as equals; and also what they talked about.

'They talked about the world. Everyone else I knew talked only about things that were near, about the village, about the harvest. But Sabri and Fatima talked about what was right and what was wrong.

'At first I did not understand much of it. But then I began to realise that often he was talking about the Pasha. Now Osman, too, often talked about the Pasha but in his house, my mother's house, the Pasha's word was law. It was: "He will want this" and "He had said that." And there was no questioning. Whereas in Sabri's house there was always questioning. And much criticism of the Pasha.

'And so I gradually began to learn about ideas and how they have an existence of their own apart from things. In time I met other people, especially through the school, and learned from them, and eventually I began to find a path on my own. But I knew that I owed it to Sabri. To Fatima also, but chiefly to Sabri.

'And then one day I heard that he was dead. The next time I was in the village I went to see Fatima, but now I found her different. She was bitter against Osman and against the Pasha. There had always been bad feeling between Sabri and Osman, going back to the time when Sabri announced that in future he was going to ride with the Bedawin. Osman said: "The village is your place, and the Pasha your master." But Sabri said: "The Pasha is not my master. The time of the Pashas has gone."

'I used to hear both sides. In my uncle's house I heard his side, in Fatima's, Sabri's. And I suppose I increasingly inclined to Sabri's side because that fitted in with what I was hearing and reading elsewhere. But it was all...unreal to me. It was something only that I heard about and read about.

'But then Sabri died and I felt Fatima's bitterness and I knew that was real. At first I could not understand it. "Why are you so bitter against my uncle?" I demanded. But she would not tell me, she said these things were not for me. And then I was angry, and I thought she was blaming my uncle without cause.

'But then one day I heard my uncle speaking to a cousin who was steward at another of the Pasha's estates, the main one where the Pasha himself lived, at Ossawa. They were talking about Sabri's death. And my uncle said: "It was necessary."

'How could it be necessary, I asked myself? *Necessary?* And I waylaid the cousin afterwards and said: "What does this mean? Why did Sabri have to die?" And he would not answer, and said it was none of my business. And I pressed him and at last he said that those who served the Pasha had to serve him for good or ill. And he would say no more.

'I went away by myself and thought about what he had said. I talked to others in the house. They told me that just before he died Sabri had been to see Osman. You know that already, and that it was about Salah. But as I went on thinking, it seemed to me that it could not have been just about Salah that they spoke, that Sabri must have said something else, something that troubled Osman greatly. For he at once sent a message to the Pasha at Ossawa, which he surely would not have done had it just been about Salah.'

'You have reasoned admirably,' said Owen, 'as I would have expected. Did you reason further?'

'Yes. I asked myself what the message could have been.'

'And?'

'Sabri was your man. He told Osman he was going to see you. He had just come back from the West. I think he brought news of the Senussi. Which Osman knew the Pasha would not want you to hear.'

⁂

'And so you decided to come to me?'

'No.'

'No?' said Owen surprised.

'No. Not at first. At least, it wasn't like that. At first I was very confused. Osman is my uncle, I have known him since I was a child. I could not believe that—that he had done a thing like this. I kept going over it in my mind, going through my reasoning again and again. It is just thought, I said to myself. It is not real. And I tried to put it away, but it would not go away.

'I wanted to talk to someone but there was no one I could talk to. My mother? But I have not talked to her for ages and she would not understand. My father? My father is greatly stricken lately, he is not the man he was—perhaps it is I who have stricken him—and he would find it hard. Fatima? She is the one I would normally go to, but she is just the one I couldn't go to on this.

And then I thought of you. You seemed to understand me. At least you listened to me.

'But then I thought, he is British, he is an enemy! I cannot go to *him*! Osman, even if he has done wrong, is on our side.

'And then another, horrible, thought struck me. Perhaps he did this *because* he is on our side. Am I now to go to the British and tell them?

'But then I thought of Sabri, and it felt as if my heart was tearing itself apart. How could I think of sides when it was Sabri? What side was Sabri on? He was on your side and against the Pasha, yes but he was not really on your side, he was on his own side, or, perhaps, Egypt's side against the both of you. And I felt as if it was not just my heart that was being pulled apart but also my mind. I *had* to have someone to talk to; so again I thought of you.

'I made up my mind, however, that although I would go to you, I would not tell you, not at once. I would talk to you first and then if it seemed that I *could* tell you, then perhaps I would. So I did not come to tell you, I came—I came to find out.'

'To find out?'

'I thought perhaps that you felt for me. A little. As a woman. And that if you did, perhaps you could come to this not as the Mamur Zapt but as—as someone outside.'

❦

She had poured it out in one continuous, passionate flow and now she sat there quietly looking at him, not exactly defiantly, and certainly not pleading, but as if conscious that she had dared and was now awaiting the consequences.

Owen took his time about replying. He didn't want to get this wrong.

'I am glad you have come to me. Not as the Mamur Zapt but as a man. And as a man, may I say that I greatly admire you for the way you have spoken. I hope you will always come to me as to a man. Over Sabri's death, however, I have to be the Mamur Zapt.'

She nodded.

'I understand that,' she said.

'It may make your mind easier to know that on Osman you have told me nothing, or very little, that I did not already know.'

'It does make it easier,' she said, after a moment.

'The little I did not know relates to the messenger. Can you tell me—you needn't if you don't want to—did the messenger come back?'

'Yes.'

'That is all I want to know.'

She stood up.

'I must go now.'

She came towards him holding out her hand.

'We shall not be able to meet again,' she said, 'like this. Not when I am a wife.'

Owen had tried several times during the morning to ring Lawrence at his office but every time he wasn't there. He came across him at lunch-time, though, in the Bar of the Sporting Club. He was talking to Curtis.

'Of course, they're everywhere,' Curtis was saying.

'Are they?' said Lawrence. He looked bored.

'Oh, yes. Place leaks like a sieve.'

'I daresay.'

He saw Owen and greeted him with relief.

'You know Curtis?'

'Oh, yes.'

Owen could see that he was going to move away and leave him landed with Curtis, so he spoke quickly.

'That message I spoke to you about, has it got through yet?'

'Yes. Even the Turks think it's barmy.'

'It doesn't matter how barmy they think it. The thing is, it's got through?'

'And that means there's a channel of communication by which it can be got through. That's what I've always said.'

'Ah, but now we know the channel.'

'You do?' Lawrence looked at his watch. 'Well, I'm glad to hear it.'

'Channel?' said Curtis. 'To the Turks? That sounds serious.'

'Not very,' said Lawrence. 'Just one of many, if what you say is true.'

'Well, of course, they're all around—'

But Lawrence wasn't listening. He detached himself without even a nod of farewell.

'Funny bloke,' said Curtis. 'One to keep your eye on, I think.'

Sabri's son was waiting for him when he got back to the office.

'I have found the man,' he said: 'the one who went from the village to the Camel Market on the day before my father died.'

'A villager?'

'He works for the Pasha.'

Owen nodded.

'You have done well,' he said. 'Now, listen. A Greek will come to your mother's house tomorrow morning. I want you to show him the man.'

'Will he kill him?' asked Salah.

'No. He is just one who helped to point the knife, not the one who pressed it home.'

'That is enough. I will kill him myself.'

'You will do no such thing. I have need of him. Leave him to the Greek and to me.'

In the Camel Market the heat was building up. The few customers had retreated beneath the trees. Most of the sellers of celluloid beads and gaudy cottons had disappeared into their makeshift lean-tos. The dark-gowned, scarred-faced village women squatting beside their pyramids of onions and mounds of grain hunched themselves even more drowsily. From behind the carpeting of the fiki's booth came a low, somnolent chant.

Over where the animals were kept there were about a dozen camels kneeling in the shade. Nearby were a few donkeys, with men squatting beside them. The only moving figure was that of the donkey-barber. From time to time he seized one of the donkeys, rather as a farmer might seize a sheep to be shorn, thought Owen, dragged it out to where there was already a large pile of clippings, and set to work.

The small boys of the Market had stopped pelting each other with camel dung and began to develop a new game, lobbing the dung instead on to the sagging roofs of the lean-tos. From time to time someone would come out and chase them away.

Georgiades was wandering thoughtfully along one of the lanes of copper pot sellers, occasionally stopping to scrutinise the vessels for washing your hands. He had a friend with him, whom he held in a warm, familiar embrace. The friend looked rather glum.

Owen continued his slow perambulation round the Market, stopping frequently to exchange a few words with the stall-holders and sellers. Eventually he made his way over to the small boys.

'Found anything this morning?' he asked.

They had. They showed him two dead, swollen rats and the gnawed carcase of a young camel, the milky fur still visible in patches. And also another baby, Leila's, they thought, though one of the boys indignantly denied this.

They asked him in turn if he had found Sabri's killer yet.

'Getting there, getting there,' said Owen. He looked back across the empty lanes of the shopping part of the Market to where Georgiades was examining the kohl bottles. 'In fact, you might be able to help me,' he said. 'You see that man with the Greek? He came to the Market on the day before Sabri was killed. Do you remember him?'

Oh, yes, they thought. They knew everybody who came to the Market, especially strangers.

'And do you remember who he talked to?'

'What is the donkey-barber,' said Anji philosophically, 'but a flea? A flea on the skin of history. The donkeys follow the great tides of history; and he follows the donkeys. The donkeys go to the wars, and he goes with them. They return, and he returns. And then, while they wait in the outer courts, he waits with them. He is never a man of the inner courts. Nor is he a warrior. He is just a man of the donkeys. As the donkey is a part of history, so is he; but only as the donkey is a part of history.'

'You are too modest,' said Owen. 'The flea does not shape history.'

'Nor, alas, does the donkey-barber.'

'Does not he sometimes take messages while he goes with the donkeys? And might not they sometimes shape history?'

The donkey-barber looked at him sharply, then smiled.

'Not the kind of messages a donkey-barber would take!'

'Again, you are too modest. What if the messages were to the Turks? Or, say, the Senussi?'

The smile faded.

'The Turks? The Senussi?'

'Telling them, perhaps, that the time had come.'

'Time for what?'

'Invasion.'

'Invasion!'

'Might not that shape the course of history?'

'It might if it were true!'

'In fact, it didn't and won't. But that is not the fault of the donkey-barber.'

'You make too much of the donkey-barber,' the man muttered.

'I do but say that he is more than a flea. Although, like the flea, there comes a moment when he must be picked off the skin.'

'It has come to that, has it?' said the donkey-barber.

'Yes,' said Owen. He nodded to Georgiades, who had come up behind the donkey-barber while they had been talking. Georgiades closed in.

'Very well, then,' said the donkey-barber resignedly, as he felt Georgiades' hands upon him, 'it has come to that.'

'However,' said Owen.

'However?' said the donkey-barber, with a glint of hope.

'Why should the fleas suffer while the great go free?'

The donkey-barber shook his head.

'I am not saying anything,' he said. 'I am just a passer of messages.'

'Again, you are too modest,' said Owen. 'Do not fleas sometimes bite?'

'Not this flea!'

'And take blood?'

'Blood?'

'Sabri's blood.'

The donkey-barber was silent for a long time. Then he said, 'How did you know?'

'It had to be someone used to animals who could go among them at night and not disturb them too greatly; and yet it was not the Bedawin. It had to be someone who knew the Market, knew it well enough to be able to work by night; and yet it was not someone of the Market, for I had eliminated all those. It had to be someone who was there that night. It had to be someone with a reason.'

'What was my reason?'

'It was less yours than the Pasha's. He knew that Sabri was going to tell me that the Senussi were going to invade and he did not want it to get to me. He sent to you because he knew you were here, where Sabri would be spending the night, and would do his bidding.'

'This is but supposition,' protested the donkey-barber.

'I have the man who brought you the message,' said Owen, looking across the Market to where the Market constables were holding Georgiades' friend. 'And I know the message.'

The donkey-barber was silent.

'And so I ask again,' said Owen: 'should the flea suffer while the great go free?'

'If you already know so much,' said the donkey-barber, 'he will not go free.'

'Your word would make the lock more certain.'

The donkey-barber shook his head.

'I will say nothing.'

'Do you so love the Pasha?'

The donkey-barber's eyes flashed.

'I do not love any Pasha,' he said. 'Much less this one.'

'And yet you do his bidding,' Owen pointed out.

'I do *not* do his bidding. I killed Sabri because—because it had to be done.'

'If you are not the Pasha's man, whose man are you?'

The donkey-barber did not reply.

'The Turks'?'

'I am no man's man. And yet I serve the Turks, yes. In this. They recruited me to carry messages. They knew I did not love the British, that I hoped for an end to British rule. And so I worked for them and did what the Pasha commanded. But not because he commanded. Nor because I love the Turks. But because a Turkish victory will see an end, not just to the British but to the Khedive. And to the rule of the Pashas. It is Egypt I fight for, the Egypt of the fellahin.'

'You think the fellahin would be free if the Turks came?'

'Not perhaps at once. We would have to fight for that, too.'

'You fool,' said Owen. 'Sabri thought like you. He wished to see an end to the Pashas. He looked beyond the rule of the British and of the Khedive to a time when the fellahin would not be bound to the land but would be their own masters, a society for which he hoped to prepare his son. He was one of your own; and yet you killed him.'

Chapter Sixteen

By the time that Owen had got back from the Camel Market and seen that the donkey-barber was lodged in the cells at the Bab-el-Khalk, it was already quite dark. Before going home he checked at his office to see if anything had come in in his absence. It had, and he sat and worked at it at his desk until quite late. When he looked at his watch it was past midnight. He jumped up with a guilty start. Zeinab would have been home long before. He shoved the papers away in his desk, put out the light and went out.

It was dark in the corridor and dark on the stairs but he found his way down to the orderly room, where there was a single light on and an orderly curled up asleep on the floor behind the desk. Owen didn't disturb him. The door was locked so he went out of a side one.

The courtyard was bright with moonlight and he was about to make his way across it when he heard something move in the shadows further along the wall.

He stayed for a moment where he was and then heard the movement again.

It would probably be beggars but he would make sure.

He went quietly towards the noise, keeping to the shadow of the wall. He couldn't quite make the movements out. It didn't sound like beggars.

He saw there was only one man and was about to step forward
when the man moved out into the moonlight and he caught
sight of his face.

It was Yasmin's brother.

He saw Owen at the same moment and gave a startled exclamation.

'What are you doing here?' said Owen, and caught him by
the front of his coat.

He tried to break away but tripped over something and
stumbled and by the time he had recovered Owen had him in
an arm-lock.

He pushed him against the wall and ran his hand over him.
He didn't seem to have a weapon.

'What are you doing here?' Owen said again.

His foot caught against something. He kicked it out into the
moonlight. It was a broken box which seemed to contain straw
and wood shavings. Owen felt around with his foot. There were
other bits of wood and something which seemed like paper. Then
his foot touched something hard and he heard the liquid move
in it and a moment after smelled paraffin.

ﻖ

'It would not have burned,' said Owen later, when he had got
him in one of the cells.

'No?'

'This is the Bab-el-Khalk. The walls are made of stone.'

'Not have burned?'

The man seemed puzzled.

'Stone.' He saw the man's vacant face and suddenly realised
that he was mentally retarded. 'Stone,' he said. 'It doesn't burn.
Not easily, at any rate.'

'Everything burns!' said the man angrily.

'Not stone. Not the Bab-el-Khalk. It's not,' he said carefully,
'like a liquor house.'

'No.' The man seemed to accept this. 'It's the alcohol,' he
said, after a moment. 'That's what burns.'

'Yes.'

'And the sin.'

'Sin?'

'Sin burns easily too.'

'Does it?'

'Yes.'

He suddenly became angry again.

'They come to our country and riot and blaspheme. They do not heed the Prophet's injunctions. They smoke and they drink and they drag us down. They must be swept away. That's what he said.'

'He? Osman?'

'Not swept away, I thought. Burned. That is what you do with bad things. Things you do not want. You burn them. Fire cleans all.'

'But why did you want to burn the Bab-el-Khalk?' And then he realised. 'Was it me you wanted to burn?'

The man stared at him in puzzlement.

'You?'

His face frowned in concentration.

'Yes, you!' he shouted.

'But why?'

'Yasmin! You were dallying with her, treating her lightly!'

Owen shook his head.

'No,' he said. 'That is not true.'

But the mind had already lost its focus.

'They come to our country like locusts,' he said, almost inaudibly, more to himself than to Owen, 'and devour our substance. They treat our women with disrespect. They dishonour us daily in the streets. Everywhere is looseness and sin.'

The voice died away and then after a moment it came again, more strongly.

'It must be burned,' he said. 'All must be burned.'

He was not seeing Owen now, he was looking past him.

'Fire!' he said. 'It is beautiful.' He was speaking dreamily, almost ecstatically. 'It sucks us in and purifies us. It destroys the husk and frees the spirit. I have seen them, you know,' he said to Owen, confidingly. 'In the flames. You see them dancing. Dancing, dancing.'

⁂

The Sekhmet family was devastated. Mrs Sekhmet collapsed at the arrests of her brother and her son. Selim had done his checking and found that Fahmy had been seen beforehand hanging around the other places where there had been fires too. Mohammed Sekhmet felt the blow just as keenly but for him, once he had recovered from the shock, there was an added burden: the disgrace. For a man like him it was unbearable. He at once resigned his position and although Owen tried to dissuade him—as did, Owen learned later, a little to his surprise, Garvin—he couldn't be persuaded to change his mind.

'They could not trust me now,' he said. 'With such a family as I have, I cannot even trust myself.'

In time the pain gave way to bewilderment.

'I cannot understand it,' he said to Owen. 'My family has always been loyal. I have always been loyal. Without loyalty, what is there?'

The issue, though, was not loyalty in itself but, in the new situation brought about by the war, loyalty to whom? The Sekhmet family had kept their loyalty but found it dividing under them. What had been single and simple had become several and under the new pressures the different constituents had pulled the Sekhmets in different directions. Osman had retained the habitual family loyalty to the Pasha and followed him in his rediscovery of his Turkishness, but Mohammed, whose loyalty had always been to the Khedive rather than to the Pasha, had remained true to the sovereign.

Mohammed's son, with all his mental difficulties, had inherited his father's religious devoutness but in his case it had propelled him towards the Turkishness of his mother's side of the family. And Yasmin, for whom the Turkish rule of the past was as much to be resisted as the British rule of the present, was moving determinedly towards a new loyalty to the Egypt that she sensed was coming.

In some ways the hardest thing for Mohammed Sekhmet to cope with was his daughter. For a long time he couldn't even speak of her. In her he saw an anticipation of all the later disasters that had fallen upon his family. From the start she had shown a disposition to stray outside the old certainties that had guided his family for generations. Was it any wonder that she had gone so badly astray? For that he blamed himself rather than her; but the remedy was obvious. It was to return her as speedily as possible to the old traditions. That meant marriage: and marriage, moreover, to someone who would see that in future she kept to the norms expected of women in her society.

Owen pleaded Yasmin's cause but got nowhere. Indeed, he began to feel that he was making things worse for her. He decided to consult Aisha.

Aisha, after consideration, said that this time she was unable to help but suggested that she ask Mahmoud.

Owen hesitated. Greatly as he liked Mahmoud, he wasn't sure he was the right man for this.

'Don't you think he might be a little too—?'

'Mahmoud takes a traditional view of the family,' said Aisha, 'and so, if you can persuade him, he is just the man to speak to Mohammed Sekhmet.'

It took a long time, and an even longer time, once he was persuaded, for Mahmoud to persuade Mohammed Sekhmet, but eventually he did. Yasmin, then, was to be allowed to resume her education, first at school and then—Well, where? Owen felt that Yasmin had a natural bent for the law. Here, though, they encountered a problem. There were no law courses for women; indeed, few courses for women at all.

Once again Labiba Latifa came to the rescue. Not in the law as such, perhaps, but some of the new courses in social work with women and children included law as part of the curriculum and could be taken by women.

And if that failed, she could always join Zeinab at the hospital annexe.

Zeinab was working terribly hard as more and more wounded soldiers poured into Egypt. Increasingly they were Egyptian, first the Camel Corps casualties from the skirmishes with the Senussi, then the Labour Corps casualties from the fighting along and across the Canal.

Work suited Zeinab. She found administration surprisingly satisfying but there was more to it than that. As an administrator she met men, both British and Egyptian, on equal terms. Under the general pressure of work old differences began to matter less.

Owen did not see as much of her as he would like; but then, neither did Faruq.

When Faruq resumed his importuning, Zeinab was simply too busy to notice.

Owen noticed, though, and in the discussion at the Intelligence Committee of the spy chain and the Pashas' role in it took the chance to point out the risks of having someone like Faruq so close to all the information that was passing through the Sultan's Office. Shortly afterwards Faruq left Cairo.

At first Owen had some difficulty in pressing charges against the Pasha Ismail. True, he had been exporting cotton illegally but the circles around the Sultan took a relaxed view of that. Wasn't everybody doing it? They took a similar view of the Pasha's links with the spy chain. Wasn't everybody doing that, too?

What about the killing, asked Owen? Was everybody doing that too?

Perhaps not. However, it was only a fellah that had been murdered and the Mamur Zapt seemed to have got the man who did the actual murdering. Why bring a Pasha into it?

Here, surprisingly, Hassan Marbri took a hand. Owen had passed all his information on to him. It was his first case and he meant to make the most of it. The Pasha was implicated in the killing of an Egyptian citizen, he insisted, and the law must take its course. The Parquet sided with its own—it didn't like the Pashas any more than it did the British—and ensured that Ismail was brought to trial. On Sabri's murder, as opposed to the espionage, the donkey-barber *was* prepared to give evidence. The Pasha Ismail was convicted along with him and after that their criminal activities came to an end.

⌘

Georgiades was now happily back on the streets. He had lost his care-worn look and seemed positively blooming. Then one day Owen came into the office and found him ashen.

'What's the matter?'

Georgiades could only shake his head dumbly.

'Something gone wrong?'

'Rosa,' Georgiades managed to gasp.

'The deal?'

Georgiades nodded his head despairingly.

'It's gone wrong?'

'It's gone right,' said Georgiades hoarsely.

'Gone *right*?'

'She's made so much money that it's indecent.'

'Well, surely—'

'All my life,' said Georgiades, 'I've been a working man. I was brought up to work. I *like* work. And although the pay's not much, it's been okay as far as I'm concerned. But now my wife comes along and makes more money in a couple of months than I'll make in the whole of my life! It's all wrong.'

'Well, I've never understood this financial stuff myself,' said Owen. 'It all seems a bit shady to me. But, look, Rosa's not shady. She's sharp, that's all. A good businesswoman, like her grandmother. There's nothing wrong with that. And, hell, she's made you rich!'

'I don't want to be rich. I want to be normal.'

'Look, it will help with the house and the kids.'

Georgiades shook his head.

'This is only the beginning,' he said. 'Now she's done it once, she'll want to do it again. She's set up a company. I'm on the board.'

'You're on the board? Christ!'

'I know. I've said to her, look, Rosa. I'm not the man for this sort of thing. No, no, you are, she said. You're just the kind of director I like: sit there, understand nothing, say nothing, do nothing. Just nod when I tell you.'

'Look, you're not going to leave?'

'Leave? Who said anything about leaving?'

'Well, you know, with all this money—'

'It's got to be ploughed back. That's what Rosa says, There's going to be no splashing around, she says. We'll live as we've always lived. Except that she's taken over half the street as offices.'

When last heard of, Rosa was selling Curtis the sand of the desert; for the cement he would be needing, she assured him, when they started building the new fortifications along the Canal.

To receive a free catalog of Poisoned Pen Press titles, please contact us in one of the following ways:

Phone: 1-800-421-3976
Facsimile: 1-480-949-1707
Email: info@poisonedpenpress.com
Website: www.poisonedpenpress.com

Poisoned Pen Press
6962 E. First Ave. Ste. 103
Scottsdale, AZ 85251

CPSIA information can be obtained at www.ICGtesting.com
Printed in the USA
LVOW111512091011

249738LV00001B/194/P

9 781590 582978